Nic screamed as she grabbed at the rocky ledge with nothing to hold on to.

"I'm not letting go. So do as I say and swing your arm around and grab hold of my arm."

Nic angled her head to look up at him. He could see the doubt she had in him in her eyes. She had no reason to trust him at all. She had no reason to believe that he would hold on. After all, he hadn't held on to her before. And suddenly, as he stared down into her fierce green eyes, Jett knew those eyes had the power to see into his past where he saw only darkness.

If he let her go now, he would never know what happened the night of the accident. Up until this moment, he hadn't realized he really wanted to know.

Jett tightened his hold on her. Rescuing Nic could be the most important rescue in his career.

Katy Lee writes suspenseful romances that thrill and inspire. She believes every story should stir and satisfy the reader—from the edge of their seat. A native New Englander, Katy loves to knit warm, woolly things. She enjoys traveling the side roads and exploring the locals' hideaways. A homeschooling mom of three competitive swimmers, Katy often writes from the stands while cheering them on. Visit Katy at katyleebooks.com.

Books by Katy Lee

Love Inspired Suspense

Visit the Author Profile page at Harlequin.com for more titles.

HOLIDAY SUSPECT PURSUIT

KATY LEE

LOVE INSPIRED SUSPENSE

INSPIRATIONAL ROMANCE

LOVE INSPIRED® SUSPENSE
INSPIRATIONAL ROMANCE

ISBN-13: 978-1-335-72272-0

Recycling programs
for this product may
not exist in your area.

Holiday Suspect Pursuit

Copyright © 2021 by Katherine Lee

This edition published by arrangement with Harlequin Books S.A.

For questions and comments about the quality of this book, please contact us at CustomerService@Harlequin.com.

Love Inspired
22 Adelaide St. West, 40th Floor
Toronto, Ontario M5H 4E3, Canada
www.Harlequin.com

Printed in U.S.A.

And if one prevail against him, two shall withstand him;
and a threefold cord is not quickly broken.

—Ecclesiastes 4:12

To my readers; we are stronger together.

ONE

Only someone who had once looked death in the face and won would dare ski such a treacherous incline. The daunting grade of the New Mexico mountain stretched steeply before her. The snow-covered terrain could barely be called a slope; it was more like the side of a cliff. Nicole Harrington locked her boots into her skis and pushed out a deep breath of vapor. And fear. Her ride up to the summit—a helicopter—had already lifted off and left her behind. There was only one way down.

Straight.

In Nic's line of work as an FBI agent, taking risks was part of her everyday life, and the summit of Wheeler Peak was nothing compared to the bullet that landed in her back eight months ago. Like a victor, she raised her arms with her poles at the ready and mentally checked for any pain in her back where the bullet had lodged in her lung.

No pain at all.

Now to convince her boss she was set to return to the daily grind. If she made it off this mountain alive, it would be all the proof she needed.

"I'm ready." She spoke aloud, as if saying it would remove any doubt.

With her body poised over the tops of her skis, her two long red braids swung forward. Her hair was tied off with bright pink elastics that matched her coat. She surveyed the un-groomed trail before her. The cold mountain air offset her adrenaline as she pushed off on the freshly fallen snow, so thick, she would sink if she didn't keep her body crouched and moving.

In her rush, her skis plowed through the top layers of snow, sending a spray of white in all directions. Her body propelled the drop at a nearly ninety-degree angle, her knees lifting to her chest as her legs turned rapidly side to side in unison. Each twist at the hip caused no back pain. If she could face this death-defying feat, then it was safe to say she was one hundred percent healed and ready to confront the dangers of her job again.

Facing death head-on was how Nic lived;

when it was her time to go, it would be how she died. The gunman who'd shot her from behind hadn't known she lived life on her own terms. He was locked up behind bars now. He had messed with the wrong agent.

Nice try, though. She took the jump off a large gray boulder and turned in a 360-degree stunt. She landed smoothly, face forward, to resume her descent. A little trick she'd learned growing up on this very mountain. She knew where all the great jumps were. The higher she flew, the better.

Nic picked up speed with precision and skill, her body healed after months in a rehab bed. She was finally ready to take on the next bad guy—the same way she took on this mountain. But before she returned to her post as a special agent, Nic had another mountain to face: her boss. If he could see her now, he'd eat crow. If only her supervisor believed she was ready, but after the last month of fruitless debates with Lewis, she felt invisible…forgotten.

Forgotten.

Nic trembled from a shiver that shot up her spine, and it had nothing to do with the morning chill or the memory of the pain in her back.

Instantly, her concentration broke as she

wondered why this fight was so important. *Am I pushing myself too hard? Is it because I'm afraid of being forgotten?*

Nic cut a sharp right to snowplow her skis to an immediate stop. This was not a slope to take without total focus. She ripped her ski mask off her face and rubbed her forehead. As if that would erase the memory of the last time she had been forgotten. No matter how far she went, no matter how far up the ladder she climbed, nothing erased the pain of that feeling. Not even a gunshot wound.

Nic shouted in frustration and heaved her poles to places unknown. She dropped backward and landed in the deep snow for an extended moment of self-pity. Her eyes closed against the bright sun and only opened when she heard the distinct chuff of the rotating blades of a helicopter overhead. It sounded close.

Was her ride coming back? She'd told the pilot not to worry about her. Perhaps he picked up another skier at the base and was heading up to the helipad at the top.

"Great," she said sarcastically and pushed up on her elbows. "So much for being alone."

Standing, she scanned the blue skies above, first to her right then to her left. The hair on the back of her neck lifted when she realized the chopper was approaching her from behind.

Nic fumbled in her skis to turn her body around to face the helicopter. It wasn't the same chopper that had airlifted her up here. This one had a yellow nose that was pointed down, completely off balance, and it quickly tilted on its side. Nic inhaled sharply. It was coming in for a crash landing on the side of the mountain!

Right where she was standing.

She kicked off her skis and tried to run. The snow pulled her boots in with every step she took. Her mad dash for a boulder twenty feet away might as well have been a million feet. She stole glances over her shoulder, believing death had finally found her.

Ten feet to go to reach the boulder and her legs were already shaking with fatigue. She lifted her booted foot out of the deep snow and pressed forward another step.

The landing skids of the helicopter brushed the tops of the trees, branches breaking with echoing cracks in the atmosphere. The collision with the tall pines slowed the chopper and tilted its white cabin onto its side. The cockpit wedged the treetops, its rotors breaking more branches as it strained against them. The pines bent under the weight; the sounds of cracking timbers echoing across the terrain around her. The chopper broke through and barreled at her in freefall.

Nic reached the boulder, taking the rock in a high leap. She didn't stop, just kept running up the rock and diving over the top.

The sound of the helicopter hitting the mountainside blared in her ears at the same time the impact's pressure momentum shoved her behind the boulder. She heard the plow of snow as the chopper swooshed forward, its blades fighting the deep layers to continue their motion. A loud crunch sounded from the other side of the rock where she hovered low.

The treetops had failed to stop the helicopter, but the boulder had triumphed.

Nic lay facedown in the snow, her arms covering her head as the mountain reclaimed its silence once again, as though something so horrific hadn't just breached its tranquility. For a moment, she wondered if she had imagined the crash. It was so surreal. Slowly, she rose, realizing she still gripped her goggles in her hand. She tossed them, needing to see to the wreckage.

And if there were survivors.

Nic ran around the boulder just as the sound of crunching metal echoed through the stillness. She came to stand in front of

the mangled chopper. The door on the side
had been thrown open. The bright sun glinted
off the smashed glass, hindering her search
for the pilot's seat. Someone sat there, still
strapped in.

Were they alive?

Who opened the door?

She took a step to find out, but a loud bang
stopped her cold.

Gunshot.

The sound ricocheted through the air—and
through her body—triggering a past incident
as though her gunshot wound was happening all over again. The memory of a shattered
rib and a punctured lung stole her breath. A
gunshot. Its echo bounced off the sides of the
peaks and scattered any remaining birds in
the trees in all directions.

Nic dropped to her knees and froze.

Officer down.

No. Helicopter down.

But why would they be firing off a weapon
if they just crashed? She had to be mistaken.
Maybe she imagined it. Maybe it was a last
backfire from the engine. Maybe she really
did need to still see the counselor. With no
time to think that one through, she pushed
herself up onto her knees, ready to offer aid
to the survivors once again.

Please let them all be alive.

Crawling forward, she came around the side of the helicopter to see a white-haired man tossing a duffel bag through the open side door. He removed a red knit hat from his back pocket and put it on. He had blood on his hands but had managed to survive the crash. She opened her mouth to call out but saw the gun tucked into the back waistband of his pants. Her words of assistance fell silent at the sight.

She'd been correct about the gunshot.

Nic glanced to the front of the helicopter. Now, from this angle, the sun wasn't blinding her. She could clearly see the pilot slumped in his seat, his blood splattered on the cockpit glass.

Blood.

How? From the crash or the gunshot?

She looked back at the white-haired man as he hefted the duffel bag onto his shoulder. Ducking when he turned, she watched him head down the mountain, skirting the tree line until he stepped up to the thick of the tall pines.

Another sound, off in the distance, caught both their attentions and lifted their gazes to the sky. A rescue helicopter was coming to the aid of the downed chopper.

Nic looked at the man at the same time he turned for the woods. Except, as he turned, he caught sight of her.

In the next second, his weapon drawn, he took aim. Two shots exploded through the mountain serenity.

Nic leaped back behind the boulder, landing with arms out as she sank deeper into a thick drift of snow. She grunted but barely heard the sound over the reverberations of the gunshots through the tall pines. The blasts blared in her head.

Her body trembled, and her face fell farther into the icy snow. The cold burned her skin, but the echoes of the gunfire froze her more than any temperature. At any second, the shooter would finish her off. She had an unloaded gun in her backpack—she never left home without it, and being up on the mountain alone, she could encounter any number of wildlife that might require defending herself. But with her lack of movement, she might as well have left it in the base lodge. She couldn't even turn around to face death head-on, never mind go for her weapon and load it. This fact collided with another fact: death drew near once again. All her bravado about being ready for work was proving itself to be a lie. With another target on her back, Nic braced for the bull's-eye.

Jett Butler let out a slow whistle from the controls of his Search and Rescue chopper. He scanned out his side window, peering through the treetops and down the mountain slope for any sign of the helicopter he had seen struggling only moments before. No sign of smoke was a good thing, but that didn't mean the aircraft wasn't mangled in the thick trees. It had to be there somewhere.

"Do you see anything on your side?" Jett asked his partner.

Tank was the best Search and Rescue K-9 a deputy could ask for up in these perilous mountains. The Siberian Husky, safety-strapped into the seat beside Jett's, lifted his snout to howl. The sound of the chopper's rotors drowned out the dog's reply, but he turned his piercing gray-blue eyes on his handler and expressed determination. Tank's black-and-white coat rippled with his flexing muscles. The dog wanted to run. The deep snow below only excited him more.

A flash caught Jett's attention. He turned the chopper ninety degrees for a better view.

Had the sun glinted off any metal?

He turned a bit more as another flash startled him…and confused him. It didn't resemble a flare, but rather…*a weapon firing?*

That made no sense, but who knew why that yellow-nosed copter had been struggling. Perhaps foul play on board had triggered its dissent.

Jett's helicopter whipped to the right, caught by the wind. A quick grab at the controls and he secured his ride. The high winds today at the summit were most likely what had caused the other chopper to crash. Even Jett, an experienced pilot, shouldn't stay in the air for much longer. Gun or no gun, he would take this bird down and continue his search on foot.

Jett pulled back on the controls and lifted the chopper higher, the landing pad as his destination. At the same time, he radioed his plans to Sheriff Stewart.

"I'm sending up Mac and Trevor for backup," the sheriff responded. "And I don't want to hear any backlash about it. You can't work alone all the time."

"I don't work alone," Jett argued and glanced his dog's way. "Tank's all the backup I need." *And the only partner I trust.* Tank never looked for more than what Jett could offer. Unlike everyone else.

The snow-covered helicopter pad neared.

"I'm bringing her down now," he informed the sheriff. "I'm not waiting for Mac and Trevor to check the scene out. If someone is shooting at someone, time is critical."

"I figured you wouldn't wait," Sheriff Stewart grumbled. "Just be careful of the mountain wave. We wouldn't want you in an accident."

Jett's headset went silent as the last word hung out there. To anyone listening, Sheriff Stewart's comment would sound like heartfelt concern from one law enforcement officer to another.

To Jett it sounded like a dig.

"Don't you mean *another* accident?" Jett corrected, referencing his car accident that left him with a traumatic brain injury.

A huff came through the headphones. "You think what you want, Jethro." The sheriff used his full first name, sounding so much like Jett's father. The two men had once been army buddies, and now Don Stewart filled a role Jett's father no longer honored. "Just because you think everyone is out to get you, doesn't make it so. Some of us do want the best for you. You suffered a lot with your amnesia. Watching you go through it was hard on everyone, but especially you. Don't fault me for caring for you. Just watch for the waves. The wind is pushing 25 knots. Storm's coming in." With that, Don signed off and Jett began his descent.

His hands tensed on the controls, feeling the wave the sheriff had mentioned. He knew full well how it felt to have no command over his life. The accident Don had alluded to had taught Jett that control was the only thing that mattered.

With the wind beneath his chopper, he had to fight hard to push through, taking aim at the landing pad. Fresh snow covered the surface, but he'd landed enough times on the summit to know where to put the craft. Perhaps the other helicopter had been trying to land and had gotten caught in the wave.

But the flash from below said otherwise.

He had to find out if it was a gun, he thought as he brought his ride down safely and securely. Jett rushed to stabilize the aircraft to shut it down. Flipping switches, adrenaline kicked in as he tore off the headset, unclipped Tank and flung the door wide.

Tank barreled out after him, sinking into the deep snow. His black tail swished back and forth, sending light powder flying.

"You're eager," Jett said, fastening the leash to Tank's blue SAR vest. "I would send you on ahead, but it might be too risky." He gave a low whistle and the two of them set out in the direction of the flashes.

The steep terrain slowed their steps in places. Jett slipped a few times, causing Tank to pause and eye him curiously. "I'm slowing you down, aren't I, boy?" Jett thought about releasing the dog to do what his breed did best in the snow. Run. When he slipped again, he nearly reached for the hook.

A blast wrenched through the mountain, sending them both into a skid. Jett caught himself from falling, but still ducked. So he'd been right about a gun.

Tank's pointed ears perked straight as he faced the direction of the shots. Judging by the volume, the shooter wasn't too far to the right.

Jett moved toward the blast but stayed in the covering of the trees. The snow depths decreased under the pine canopies, offering them less to trudge through. His steps picked up and Tank pulled him forward, straining against the leash to find the danger. "There's no fear in you," Jett whispered, pride for his partner swelling in his chest. He couldn't think of a better one to have. He ignored the fact that he chose to work alone because he was the one who didn't play well with others.

They neared a clearing but stayed in the shadows to survey the scene in front of them. Abutting a large boulder, mangled helicopter parts littered the snow. Jett glanced up to see the broken tree branches overhead. The forest had broken the descent.

But who was shooting...and why?

Jett moved to his left with silent steps across fresh snow. Thankfully, the covering hadn't hardened enough to crunch beneath his boots. He put his fingers to his lips to remind Tank to keep quiet. The dog obeyed, but remained focused on his destination.

Had Tank seen something?

Jett crouched to Tank's level and moved to the dog's line of sight.

A splash of bright pink caught Jett's eye. He crawled forward until he could make out a person in a pink jacket leaning up against the base of a tree and half buried in the snow. The person sat completely still. He wondered if they had been shot.

He reached for his sidearm, unclasping its holder. Removing the weapon, he gained his feet and moved forward. As he came around the boulder, he saw the back of a man wearing a red knit hat. He had a black leather bag. Cash looked to be overflowing from it.

Search and Rescue was in Jett's blood, but

the scene before him appeared more nefarious than a helicopter crash. Something else had gone down here. A bad drug deal, perhaps?

The sound of another chopper cut through the air.

Backup was arriving.

The man lifted a gun and pointed it in the vicinity of the person at the tree.

Jett lifted his gun and took aim at the gunman. He opened his mouth to instruct him to drop his weapon, but the helicopter came around the mountain peak, and the man lowered his gun. He took off running under the trees where the snow wasn't so deep, hefting his leather duffel over his shoulder.

Tank whined to go after the person in the snow.

Jett figured the gunman wouldn't get far on foot, and it would be safer to wait for the other deputies to take him down.

He needed to check the person in the pink coat. He watched the gunman head down the mountain in the direction of the base. As soon as he crested the next mound, Jett let Tank go, saying, "Move." The dog ran full-steam for the person in the snow.

With his gun still at the ready, Jett followed. "Put your hands where I can see them!" he commanded.

No response or movement. Not even when Tank leaped on the person. Perhaps Jett was too late, and this rescue was really a recovery.

TWO

Nic had no idea how much time had gone by since she'd landed in the snow and scurried off to hide from the flying bullets. With each bang, paralyzing fear took over her body and froze her every movement. The increasing wind tossed more snow on top of her, freezing her even more. She felt herself being buried, but her choking past trauma inside her held her in its grip and in her hiding spot against a tree. How long would it be before the man found her and finished her off?

I can't die here.

I have no physical wound.

Get up before it's too late.

The thoughts replayed in her mind for the hundredth time, at war for first place against the sound of the gunshot. Over and over, she heard the blasts, and no amount of covering her ears ended the painful sound. Literal pain ached through her back and into her left lung, reminiscent of another time.

It's not real.

But her body proved to be her worst enemy. Her mind locked on a past moment of terror that owned her. She knew the signs. She knew what the shrink would say. *Post-traumatic stress.* But what if the threat was real? What if there really was someone shooting at her? That it wasn't in her convoluted mind?

If that were the case then, where was the shooter? Why hadn't he finished her off? Why was the only sound blaring in her mind from a year ago?

Please, God, make it stop! I can't think or rationalize what's real and what's not.

Her right forearm was tugged away from her ear. Nic fought back in a frenzy to keep from being touched or taken. Her arm came free, and she tried to scuttle in the opposite direction. The snow kept her locked in place. Then she felt flurries around her, and she dared to open her eyes.

A dog was digging her out, scattering the snow away.

Did the dog belong to the shooter? But then, where was he?

The dog returned and shoved a warm nose into the crook of her neck. Nic let go of her head and touched the animal, sinking her fingers into the deep pelt. Slowly, the repeated blasts in her mind subsided and her breathing decelerated.

The cold snow also began to hurt her face. It was interesting how physical pain subsided when emotional pain took precedence. She tried to rise on one hand to get out of the snow.

"Stay still." A deep male voice spoke from above.

Nic fell back, shrinking away from the sound. Her arms flung up to protect her head even as the voice caught her attention and she tried to place it.

"I'm not going to hurt you. I'm head of Search and Rescue, and I used to be a deputy. I still work closely with the department. My name's Jett."

No, it couldn't be.

Nic lowered one arm and looked up at the man crouched low over her. Black hair, a light scuff of facial hair and piercing blue eyes… and a familiar scar below his right eye. He'd gotten it in a skiing accident…with her. He was speaking to her, but she heard nothing when his lips moved.

Jett is here. Jett's come to help me.

Nic raised both arms, this time to reach out to Jett Butler.

Ten years had passed since she'd been this close to him. How many times had she prayed he would come back to her?

And now he is here!

"You're safe," he assured her. "Were you shot?"

Nic shook from the cold. Her teeth chattered. All she could do was nod repeatedly as he lifted her off the ground. She buried her face into his shoulder.

"Where were you hit?" he said, feeling her arms and leaning back to examine her head.

It dawned on Nic that he meant right now. Not an old wound, but a fresh shot.

"N-no, n-not hit."

He sighed. "Good, but I need to get you out of the cold. Temps are dropping with a storm brewing, and the winds are picking up."

"Th-thank you f-for c-coming," Nic said and looked up to face him head-on. She couldn't believe after all he had said to drive her away, he would come to her rescue today.

"Not a problem, ma'am. It's my job."

"M-ma'am?" Nic flinched at the impersonal word. A term for a stranger.

"Sorry, didn't mean to offend. What is your name?"

Nic stiffened and tried to pull away, the cold slap of rejection practically burning her frozen cheek.

He still doesn't remember me. The car accident that had left him with amnesia a decade ago had never released his memories. That meant he still didn't know who she was.

And he hadn't come to help *her*, either.

As he'd said, he was just doing his job.

He guided her up the mountain, asking her name again. Nic held her tongue, not wanting to know if he had forgotten her name, too. After the accident she had tried to make him remember her.

"What happened to the shooter?" she asked instead. "I believe he shot the pilot after the crash. I didn't see it, but I heard it."

"He ran down the mountain." Jett glanced behind them. "He had a bunch of cash in a bag and took off. Two deputies are landing their chopper now and will go after him. He won't get far. It's a big mountain."

"I know," she replied. "I grew up on this mountain."

"You did?" Jett paused to look down at her. His blue eyes narrowed. His lips parted on a puff of air. His throat convulsed. "Come on, I need to get you to the chopper and some warm air."

I think he knows who I am now.

Nic compressed her lips at the fact that Jett didn't admit to recognizing her. The first time was innocent. This time was sheer avoidance.

Nic stepped out of the hold he had around her shoulders, guiding her. "I need to go after the shooter. He's armed and dangerous." She shrugged out of her backpack and unzipped the side compartment.

"You can't be serious."

"I'm FBI," she snapped, withdrawing her personal 9mm weapon. "Just point me in the direction he took off in and be sure to inform your deputies I'm one of the good guys. I don't need to be shot at again today."

She shivered from more than the cold but was determined not to have another trauma-response episode. She hoped it had been a one-time thing. Her supervisor, Lewis, could never know about it or she would never be able to return to work.

And Jett Butler didn't need to know about her forced leave from the Bureau, either.

"The only place you're going is back to my helicopter. This is my jurisdiction, and you aren't chasing down anybody on my mountain."

Nic loaded the magazine with 9mm rounds. She faced him and raised her chin to be sure he saw her full-on. "You're wrong on two counts. One, I am going after this guy." She inserted the magazine in place. "And two, this is *my* mountain. My father owns Wild Mountain Resort. And my name, if you haven't figure it out yet? Nic Harrington." She turned to leave but called over her shoulder before she took two steps, "Your ex-fiancée, in case you forgot that, too."

Jett rubbed his chilled cheek from the whipping wind and pulled up his neck warmer as he watched Nicole put distance between them.

Nicole Harrington. His ex-fiancée. The woman he was supposed to spend his life with—up until the car crash. Now, he had no memory of their time together. *Had she always been so...difficult?*

His initial response to the woman he had been engaged to was best kept to himself, but Nicole Harrington sure did have a cutting edge to her demeanor that concerned him.

Don't let the cute braids fool you.

He watched her trudge through the deep snow, going after the shooter. He knew he had to stop her, but part of him wished Mac and Trevor had arrived already to do the honors. He could leave her up to them. He also needed to inspect the helicopter and check the status of the pilot.

With an annoyed shake of his head, Jett called out to the woman, "Nic...ah, Miss..." He sighed, not knowing what to call her. He knew she had been a part of his life, but he had zero personal recollection of her, only what his family had told him during the early days after the car crash. So many picture albums had been thrust in his face until he'd finally put an end to all attempts to make him remember. Eventually, they'd all given up on him, and everyone had gone their own separate ways.

Something he wished he could do now.

But he had a job to do.

He noticed her glove in the snow and scooped it up. After putting it under Tank's nose, he touched the dog's head. "Stop her. No contact," he instructed Tank with a whistle. "Move." He waved his dog forward.

Jett followed behind his sprinting K-9 as Tank bulldozed through the snow at a fast clip. The husky's muscled legs lifted him up and over as he approached the woman, kicking up snow in his racing around her. She moved to pass him, but Tank jumped in her way again. Each of her moves was met by a countermove of a driven dog under orders. There was no way she would get by him.

Jett made his way to her. "I can't let you go after the suspect."

"You don't have a say. Now, call off your dog," she demanded, pointing her gun at the ground. She waved her other hand in the shooter's direction. "He is getting away."

"As an affiliate of the sheriff's department, I do have the right *and* the jurisdiction. You do not. Put the gun away, unless you want me to confis—"

A blast through the air cut him off. The whoosh of sound that flew by his head made him forget what he was about to say. "Get down!" he ordered Nic, jumping toward her to take her to ground. The loose snow pulled them in, clearing their view from the shooter. Their faces were an inch apart. Her eyes widened in fear, or was it pain? "Were you hit?"

No response.

"Nic, I need to know if you were struck." He shifted to search for any blood. None that he could see. He felt her padded jacket, full of down feathers. No sign of a single tear. He reached for her cheek and patted her. "Hey, are you all right?"

Nic jolted, and her eyes blinked a few

times. Then they narrowed on him. She pushed at his chest. "Get away!"

"Stay down," he countered.

"I told you. I am an FBI agent. I can handle myself. There is an active shooter on my mountain. I have to stop him before an innocent skier is killed. There's no other choice."

He couldn't say she was wrong, and she *was* a federal agent. "Any other circumstances, I would say no." He rolled away but still stayed low. "The shot came from the trees on the right."

Nic sidled up beside him. "Then we stay to the left for cover."

His thoughts exactly, but he didn't say anything. Partnering was not typical for him. Suddenly, she was up and running through the trees, leaving him behind. Tank rose on his front paws, his ears perked as they watched her put herself in the line of danger.

"I hope I don't regret this, but it's not looking good so far. Stay low," he instructed his dog and followed the woman in a race for cover in the trees.

Shots fired, splitting the bark of the tree ahead of him. "Nic!" he called and jumped behind it.

No response.

Jett pointed ahead. "Find her and stay with her."

The dog took off, keeping to the trees, tracking the disrupted snow from her boots.

Jett radioed Mac and Trevor. The two deputies had already set down at the crash site.

"The pilot's been shot," Trevor told him. "Looks like a deal gone bad. There're a few hundred-dollar bills scattered about."

"I saw a guy stashing money in a bag," Jett relayed.

"Do you have eyes on the suspect?"

"I'm working on it." Jett surveyed the snow in the shooter's direction.

"Well, work faster. The guy could disappear in these mountain forests."

"Nobody knows the terrain better than me," he said, then thought of the woman racing straight for the gunman. "Well, maybe one other person does, but something seems off with her."

"Her?" Trevor asked. "How so?"

Jett withheld a name. "She's frozen twice when shots were fired." He peered through the forest. Nic would be a sitting duck if she froze again.

Search and rescue took on a new meaning in that instant. Typically, the mountain's treacherous elements stood in his way of succeeding in his searches. As harsh as nature could be, he didn't typically have to ward off bullets.

Another gunshot echoed through the air. It came from farther down the mountain. Jett ran tree to tree, trying not to make himself a target, and hoping Nic was doing the same.

THREE

Get it together, Harrington. Nic held her gun at the ready and watched it shake in her trembling hand. A tree trunk shielded her view from the shooter, but as soon as she stepped out from behind it, another bullet could find her.

She pulled at her fleece neck covering, drenched not only with perspiration from running, but also from her growing anxiety. Her erratic breathing needed to get under control. This was no time to revisit the day she'd turned her back on a gunman. Not when there was another one taking aim at her right now.

Twice already, gunshots had immobilized her, ceasing all her ability to function and even to reason her way out of it. Was this what Lewis had meant when he'd said she wasn't ready to return to work? Judging by the uncontrollable paralyzing fear, would she ever be ready?

I have to be.

Nic inhaled deeply and let the air out slowly. *I will be.*

The image of the farmhouse kitchen flashed in her mind. The day when a perp's bullet plunged into her back. The undercover clothes she had been wearing may have hidden her identity, but the clothes hadn't fooled the shooter. He had known he'd have to take her out to get to the man she'd been protecting. She'd taken a bullet that should have killed her, but worse, she'd let her charge be taken. She'd failed big-time.

Never again.

The vow settled her breathing to a more natural pace. This shooter was heading for the base of the mountain. Hundreds of skiers could be in danger if this guy felt cornered. She had to do everything she could to capture him before he hurt innocent people.

"Nic!" the familiar voice of Jett Butler called out on a harsh whisper.

Her breath snagged at the sound. *Why had Jett been the first responder?* Why couldn't it have been one of the deputies she used to work with when she was in the department? Maybe Trevor or Mac, if they were still there?

She would even have taken Sheriff Stewart, even though the two of them hadn't parted on the best of circumstances. But sticking around hadn't been an option for her after the accident.

And it wasn't now.

Nic ignored Jett's call and eyed the next tree for cover. Her ski boots slowed her down, so she needed to consider gauging for time. Everything would take twice as long.

A lot could happen in four seconds.

"Nicole!" Jett called again. The way he said her name felt off. Had he ever called her by her full name?

No. Not ever. He'd called her Nikki.

She brushed off the displeasure of his use of her full name and took a step toward the next tree, but before she could put her foot down, something hit her back at full force. She fell flat on her stomach just as another gunshot exploded through the air.

The snow hit her face, its depth barely catching her fall as she sank deep. Once again, her heart raced at the sound, but this time she'd felt the hit. Had she taken another bullet in her back? She tried to turn over, but a weight held her down. She looked up and noticed the tree trunk splintered right where she would have been standing.

"Keep her down." Jett spoke. It was an order, but not to her.

His dog.

A wave of relief swept over her when she realized it hadn't been a bullet that had struck her. It had been the husky. "Call off your dog." She gave her own orders.

A gunshot sounded right above her. Nic jolted but couldn't jump with the weight of the animal on her back. She squeezed her eyes shut, but when another shot came, she cried out, "Stop! Just stop!"

Silence followed. Suddenly, the only sound she could hear was her own crying. Hot tears mixed with icy crystals, melting the snow around her face. She tried to get control of the wails, but they came from someplace deep within her.

Then she felt Jett kneel beside her. The weight on her back was removed, but the weight of her fear kept her down. "I'm ruined," she cried quietly. Only a year ago, she had risen up in the FBI to supervisor status, taking on bad guy after bad guy. She felt Jett's hand on her shoulder.

"Nicole, I need to get you to safety."

His unfamiliar name for her couldn't have come at a worse time. How easily he had forgotten her. How easily the FBI would forget her.

She sniffled, not allowing his use of her full name to stop her from protecting innocent people. "Is the shooter still around?"

"No, he went deeper into the woods. He's heading across the crest of the mountain, not down."

She let out a deep sigh. "Thank God," she said, and meant it. "He can't go near the skiers."

"I know. He won't. I'll get a team together. We'll catch him. Are you hurt?" He felt her arms, but as soon as he touched her leg, she jumped away from his reach.

"I'm fine. When do we go after him? We can't wait too long. A storm's coming. We'll lose the tracks."

"Sorry, Nicole, but you will be getting on my helicopter and going home. This is a matter for local law enforcement. And as Search and Rescue, it's my job to make sure you are safe."

"Will you stop calling me Nicole? It's Nic. It's always been Nic." *Or Nikki, for you.*

"I'll try to remember that," he said and scanned beyond the trees. "It's safe to make it back to the helicopter." He helped her stand then made a call on his radio.

With his back to her, Nic listened to him discuss a course of action with the other deputies.

"I believe I clipped him with my last shot. He took off right after that. He won't get far," Jett said.

Nic peered out from behind her tree and scrutinized the ones on the other side of the ski trail. Each passing second, the man got farther away.

"We can't wait," she said.

He let go of the radio at his shoulder and turned a stern glare her way. "I thought I made this clear. There is no *we*."

His words knocked the air from her lungs. They were the same words he'd said to her ten years ago when she'd told him they would get through his amnesia together. That she would take care of him. *We will do this together*, she'd pleaded. His vacant stare had been answer enough.

So easily forgotten.

Nic squeezed her eyes shut on the painful memory and replied, "Yeah, you made that clear. There is no we."

He scanned the tree line, oblivious to how his words affected her, how they'd brought back their past relationship. He had no idea how the two of them had had big plans to work side by side in law enforcement, protecting the town and mountain. They would have been a real power couple…until that car had hit them and ended those plans in an instant.

Jett's radio chirped from where it was clipped to the collar of his jacket. He whistled for his dog to head back up the mountain. "The helicopter, Tank."

Tank. After having the weight of the SAR dog on her, she thought the name fit him, but he was actually not a big dog at all.

A male voice spoke through the radio. Trevor Mirabel's, she believed it to be.

Jett nodded for her to start walking as he turned away to answer the call.

He had given her an order just like the one for his dog. At least he hadn't whistled.

She took a step, but not toward him. She hoped to be long gone before he realized she'd gone in the opposite direction. It had been a long time since she worked with this team, and that streak wouldn't end today. Jett had said there was no "we," and she would abide by that.

"Are you telling us you came face to face with Nic Harrington up here, and you're still *alive*?" Deputy Trevor Mirabal lowered his camera and stared at Jett. "Wait, I need to capture this moment." The deputy smirked and lifted his camera again, pointing the lens Jett's way instead of on the crash site.

Jett turned away, denying the man his photo opportunity.

Trevor moaned. "Aw, man, come on. You're never any fun."

Jett grunted under his breath and remembered again why he worked solo. He looked back down the mountain. "She was right behind me. I told her to get to the helicopter."

Deputy Mac Donnell stepped out from inside the helicopter. "Just like Sheriff Stewart told her to accept desk duty right before she walked out ten years ago. When that woman had a perp in her sights, she was unstoppable. Giving her orders never worked. She gave us orders." Mac removed his rubber gloves. "The pilot was shot execution style. Probably didn't even see it coming after surviving the crash. I'll run the tail number to see who owns this aircraft. But you're going to have to make nice with Nic. She's our only possible witness."

Trevor said, "She's 0 for 2 now."

Jett shot Trevor a look to silence him further, but the man just huffed and said, "It's true. She was in your car accident. If I were you, I'd want to know what she remembers from that night. This could be your chance to find the driver. Jett, that person took everything away from you. And not just your memory."

"I don't need to remember anything, and this conversation's over," Jett ordered.

Trevor just shrugged and went back to his pictures.

The deputy snapped photos of something in the snow. He raised the camera to study the digital image. "I got a good boot print. We'll make a cast of it to see if we can locate the make and style. Hopefully will lead to the sale and buyer."

Jett could see the men had things under control here at the scene. As Search and Rescue, his job was to go after the woman. They needed her to remember any details she might have seen during the crash and after.

"Don't be so mean to her this time," Mac called, a fingerprinting kit in his hands. "Radio if you need us to take your helicopter down and bring it to the hangar."

Trevor added, "Or if you need us to rescue you from her."

The two deputies laughed. They thought they were so funny.

Jett ignored them and whistled for Tank to follow him. It could be hours before they reached the base. He quickly found the woman's ski boot tracks and started tracking them. She was moving fast, or as fast as she could in heavy boots. He raced along with Tank, expecting to see her come into view any second.

One crest led down to another, and still no sign of her. She was hauling.

Then her tracks stopped.

Jett came to an abrupt halt. Pristine, untouched snow spread out before him, its ice crystals sparkling in the sunlight in a false peacefulness. He turned in a complete circle but found no other tracks.

She couldn't have vanished into thin air. That wasn't possible. But where could she have gone?

He looked to the edge of the trail to see if she had jumped into the woods. No evidence suggested it. Had she backtracked, placing her boots into her impressions?

Jett knew that had to be the answer.

But why?

Because she had wanted to go after the shooter and had known he wouldn't have let her.

He reached into his pocket and withdrew her glove. He put it under Tank's nose.

"Find," he said and signaled to the dog to go forward. "Move."

Tank sniffed around and made his way up the mountain. Jett had been correct. She hadn't passed this point. The foolish woman had gone after an armed killer alone. Jett wondered what she needed to prove, and to whom.

He radioed Trevor. "I hope you brought another crime scene kit. We may have a double murder by the time the sun goes down."

"Nic's?" Trevor asked.

"She went after the killer alone. Who does that?"

"Man, I'm sorry," Trevor said.

"For what?" Jett paused at the deputy's condolence.

"Um…well, you know, she did mean something to you at one point. I just thought you might be upset—"

Jett cut this preposterous idea off right away. "You thought wrong. If Nicole wants to get herself killed, that's on her. The only thing I will be upset about is breaking the news to her father. Les doesn't need another loss."

Tank barked up ahead, looking back at Jett before entering the woods on the left side.

"Good boy. Gotta go. I have a lead." Jett ended the radio call and raced up to his dog. Together, they went into the trees and picked her track up again. She must have swept the others clean, knowing he would come after her.

Tank stopped and whimpered.

"You okay, buddy?" Jett approached cautiously, wondering if the husky had stepped in a trap. If that woman had set a snare for his dog, Jett would...

Blood. And a lot of it.

The disturbed snow, sets of prints, and broken branches evidenced a tussle. The amount of blood indicated that one or both persons had been hurt. He noticed a large boulder smeared with blood. Below it, on the ground, was a swatch of something pink. A piece of Nicole's jacket, as bright as the crimson on the snow.

And just as disturbing.

Jett hit his radio, about to do something he rarely did. "Trevor, Mac, I'm going to need help down here. Now."

FOUR

A sniffing sound in Nic's ear stirred her awake. She tried to move her hand, but it felt frozen by her side. Her fingers wouldn't bend. In fact, they felt like they weren't even attached to her any longer. She opened her eyes to see snow all around her and in the trees above. She seemed to be right where she had landed when the shooter had thrown her down. She groaned, knowing she'd had him apprehended moments before his final blow had knocked her unconscious.

How long had she been out? The concern inched its way through her numbness. And where was the guy now?

She couldn't feel Tank's wet nose touching her face, only hear his snorts, and above her the sky had darkened to late afternoon. Attempting to push up on her elbows made the treetops swirl. She gave up and fell back against the rock she had landed on. She didn't have to touch the back of her head to know it was swollen with an egg-size contusion. She winced, grunting at the growing pain settling in.

At least she was still alive.

Tank lifted his snout and barked twice. His handler would be along shortly, Nic supposed. She wouldn't let Jett find her like this. She managed to roll over onto her side, but nausea arose instantly. She moaned and swallowed hard. Peering through slitted eyes, she tried to place her location on the mountain. Growing up on the resort didn't mean she knew every square foot of the slopes, but she figured she had been able to force the guy down to at least the halfway point on the west side. She tried to gauge the direction the killer retreated to and remembered seeing him limp off into the woods before she passed out. His hunched back told her he was hindered by his injuries.

She touched her jacket and felt for her weapon, sighing when she found it. She also had his gun, having confiscated the revolver and emptied it of any remaining bullets farther up the mountain. There would be no more shooting by this guy today. Already she could think clearer without having that threat at the base of the mountain.

He still has to be found, though.

Nic forced herself to a sitting position. The world tilted and the trees bent. She grabbed at her roiling stomach and closed her eyes. Her hand found the dog's collar, and she gripped hard to steady herself. Tank's strong stature helped her get to her knees. The looming trees spun around her, and she let her forehead fall to the soft fur on Tank's back.

"Nic! Oh, thank God." The sound of Jett's voice traveled to her ears, but she couldn't lift her head to see which direction he came from. She felt a hand on her back. "Where are you hurt?"

"My head," she mumbled. "I landed on the rock."

His hand touched her head. "I see a small gash. Nothing too serious. So where else are you bleeding from?"

"Bleeding?" Nic lifted her head and found Jett searching her visually for wounds. She glanced around and inhaled at what she saw.

Blood all around.

Where she had lain unconscious, red snow spread from the spot. She was bleeding from somewhere. But how?

Nic thought of when she had snuck up on the killer as he'd waited in the trees to take another shot. Her surprise attack had quickly turned into hand-to-hand combat. Anyone could be skilled with a gun, but the guy had lacked any fighting abilities. She'd had the upper hand, confiscating his weapon before he'd even known what had hit him.

Nic looked down at her blood-covered ski boots. His blood, she knew. Jett had wounded him already, but her fighting kicks with the heavy boots had opened him up. Once she'd had him apprehended, she'd prepped to lead him down the mountain.

She looked down at her shredded pink jacket and suddenly remembered what came next.

"He had a knife," she said, remembering his sneak attack. He'd come back swinging. She hadn't been expecting the knife. His assault could have been detrimental. Thankfully, her down jacket had taken most of the slice, but she could clearly see the blood now seeping from her upper thigh through her ski pants. She'd been cut. "I'm fine," she said, swooning.

"I'll be the judge of that," Jett said. He took her shoulders gently in his hands and leaned her down.

Nic shoved him back and struggled to her feet, wincing with pain as she took her first step to go after the guy. Her leg buckled. She caught herself on Jett's waiting arm.

Her numbed body from the cold snow worked against her. Her leg wound would slow her down, but knowing the shooter also had a knife motivated her. She may have his gun, but he was still a threat.

If he bled out, would he die before he reached the base of the mountain?

Wishful thinking.

She needed to apprehend him before he came into contact with a skier.

"We have to go after him. A hostage situation could arise." She took one step before losing her footing again.

"There is a team coming up from the base." Jett steadied her. He radioed his location and requested a first-aid snowmobile with a stretcher. "You will bleed out if you take any more steps. Lean on me and give your leg a rest."

Nic eyed the bloodied trail the guy took, but her cumbersome ski boots wouldn't let her take one step, never mind run. She wasn't going anywhere. The idea of being taken off this mountain on a stretcher just made everything worse.

Check that. The idea of being taken off this mountain on a stretcher by Jett was the nail in the coffin.

"I had him," she said. The frustration in her voice came through.

"And you almost made it down," Jett said as he removed a rolled-up thermal ground cover sheet from his backpack. He shook it out and placed her on it.

Nic scanned the area again. "It looks like I'm at the halfway point on the west side. That's not 'almost' to the base."

"You're wrong. It's obviously been a long time since you've been here. Just over the next hill is Smugglers Trail, which leads right down to the lodge."

Nic didn't know which was worse: being unfamiliar with her mountain or Jett's gentle ministrations as he cut her ski pants and cared for her wound. Both irked her. Ten years ago, she would have known where she was. Ten years ago, she would have been the one caring for him. He hadn't allowed her to then, so she wondered why she should allow him to now.

She watched him cinch the tourniquet on her leg. His every touch was deliberate and skilled. He may have lost his memory of her, but he hadn't lost his expertise in emergency response. With his head bent low, his black hair fell to shield his eyes from her. He wore a blue knit cap with a Search and Rescue patch and pinned to his blue parka was his Search and Rescue badge.

But no deputy badge.

"I know you used to volunteer for SAR, but why did you leave the sheriff's department?"

His hands on her leg paused. "I never went back," he said and continued stabilizing her wound.

This bit of information was news to Nic. She had left the department to avoid working with him when he was well enough to return. But maybe he forgot more than other people with his amnesia.

Maybe he forgot how to be a cop.

The motor of a snowmobile could be heard cresting the hills below them. Her ride was almost here. Soon, she would be out of his hair once again. This could be the last time she ever saw him again.

"I know you don't remember me, or us, but when I was in the department, we had plans to work this mountain town together. Catching criminals and saving people. Whether you're on the force, or not, I'm glad to see your talents didn't go to waste. You're good at your job." Nic sighed and looked in the direction the shooter had gone. "I know it doesn't look like I succeeded here today, but I'm also good at my job. I always catch my bad guys, and I'm not going to let this cut stop me."

Jett sat back on his haunches. He scanned her from her feet to her head, searching for any other wounds. The snowmobile with the stretcher attached to its side pulled up outside the tree line. "Your ride is here. An ambulance will be waiting at the base to take you to the hospital. You will need stitches, but you'll live. Make sure they look at your head. I can't see inside your skull to know if your brain has been affected."

He would know firsthand the fragility of the mind. His off-the-cuff remark took her by surprise. His whole life had been upended because of his head injury.

Which meant hers was, too.

"It's going to hurt for a few days, but I'm sure I'm fine." Nic had no time for recuperation. Already she would be delayed in finding this guy because of a few stitches.

"Just don't get any ideas." Jett stood to meet the riders on the two medic snowmobiles. He walked away before she could set him straight.

The riders were dressed in full rescue gear, their bright red coats alerting skiers to their roles of emergency response. They quickly had her secured on the stretcher and were readying to take her to the mountain base.

Jett met Trevor, and the two of them were making plans about the crash site and setting up a base camp for the investigation. Nic had to set the record straight before she was taken away. "Stitches won't take too long. I'll be back to assist the department as soon as I can."

Before either of them could dissuade her, the snowmobile headed off down the mountain at a safe but steady pace.

The terrain opened wide as they descended, the snowy ski trail smoothing out beneath her. Nic could hear the first skiers as they whisked by them. From her prostrate position, she could only see them after she passed, but she scanned the area for the shooter anyway. He was out there somewhere and, with each skier that raced past her, she hoped people would be moving too fast to be caught and hurt by this guy.

She vowed to fight to her death to uncover just what he was doing on her mountain.

She hadn't prayed in years, giving up when her prayers all held a similar connotation that reflected the thrashing her life had taken. *Why do I have to fight for everything?* It was always why, why, why. But a pity party never accomplished anything.

Been there, done that. It doesn't work.

Regardless, Nic took a deep breath and prayed for the safety of any person who crossed this man's path. She didn't understand why she was being stopped from returning to work at the FBI, or today in catching this guy, but she didn't expect a reason from God, and so she said a few words for others instead. He never answered her prayer for herself, but as Nic lay there, alone, tied onto a stretcher, she hoped He would answer her prayers if they were for someone else.

"I'm calling off the search for the night. There is no sign of the suspect, and it's too risky to have people on the mountain with the dropping temps," Sheriff Stewart said. His arms were crossed at his chest, his legs slightly parted. His stance left no room for negotiation.

"We can't call off the search," Jett said, standing his own ground, too. "The guy is bleeding out."

"The sun is down. We'll try again at dawn."

"He won't last the night."

Stewart rubbed his forehead and sighed. "Look, I know you want to take this guy in."

"I want justice," Jett corrected him. "He killed a man, but he also is up to something criminal. If he's using our mountain for drug running, don't you want to know?"

"Of course I want to know. I have a responsibility to know. I have a dead pilot with a gunshot to the back of his head. The guy never saw it coming. That tells me we're looking for someone that has no moral code. I'm not sending my men up that mountain in the cold, dark night to find a man who won't think twice about killing them. We will search in the morning and that's final."

The sheriff returned Jett's as he used his own radio to call off the search for the night. "We're setting up a base camp in the lodge. The search resumes at 6:00 a.m.," he told his deputies, adding, "Les Harrington is providing rooms for all law enforcement. The resort is temporarily closed, all skiers removed from the premises. Come get warm as we map out the plan for the morning."

Jett glanced in the direction of the multi-floored wood lodge, its tall glass windows glowing. The massive fireplace inside was circular and in the center of the lobby. Rustic wooden chairs and couches surrounded it on all sides. The view should have been inviting, but Jett knew somewhere inside Nic waited.

He'd learned that she had been stitched up and refused any other treatment. She still believed she would have a place in this investigation. He questioned why the sheriff hadn't set her straight, but he was glad to see Don had assigned Trevor to partner up with her—or more like keep an eye on her. Jett wondered how she'd reacted to having Trevor as her guardian when she returned to the lodge. At least Don had listened to him and done this. Jett may not be a deputy anymore, but he had the sheriff's ear.

After the accident ten years ago, Don was the only one who hadn't pushed him to remember anything. He accepted Jett as he was and came alongside him to get him back on his feet. Being a cop wasn't an option with a traumatic brain injury, but he could handle Search and Rescue. Don pulled clout, and the new Jett was born. The sheriff treated Jett better than his own father had. Jett barely spoke to his family anymore. They couldn't handle the fact that Jett wasn't the same person they knew him as before the hit and run. They couldn't handle the fact that they meant nothing to him.

And neither could Nic.

Jett clenched his jaw, knowing he had a fight ahead of him with her, but he wouldn't risk her heading back up the mountain and becoming another casualty. He doubted she would keep her thoughts to herself about his request to give her a babysitter and expected an earful when he got inside. He'd let her speak her peace. Then he'd give her the order to remain under watch. As his only witness, she was in a lot of danger. And as the sheriff said, this guy wouldn't think twice of putting a bullet in her head.

The heavy wooden door to the lodge clunked closed behind him and his dog. The smells of the burning fire mixed with the slightly musty odor of the older upholstery of the furniture and rugs. The evidence of many years of dripping wet skiers clomping around the lobby in their ski boots also included the scrapes and gouges in the wide-board floors. Wild Mountain Ski Resort had seen better days at its peak, but no matter the wear and tear on the place, Jett breathed in the aroma of comfort that the old place offered him. He couldn't explain why this lodge, in particular versus the other resorts in the area, drew him in, but it did. Only, as he took that breath of comfort, the view of Nic sitting by the fire with her leg up on the stone hearth staunched the effect of the ambience and made him want to retreat. After commanding Tank to rest by the door, he headed in Nic's direction.

Jett also searched for Trevor. The deputy was supposed to be sticking to Nic like glue.

"He went to get me something to drink," Nic said. She crossed her arms in front of her and tilted her head up defiantly. "He won't be back for at least twenty minutes."

"How do you know that?" Jett had yet to take a step toward her.

"I told him I was craving a Hot Chile Chocolate. It's been a long time since I've had a New Mexico favorite. He'll have to make it from scratch. Pop has been cutting corners and took it off the menu. It's been instant-only for him lately." She looked around the cavernous room and wrinkled her nose. "By the looks of the place, the menu isn't the only thing he's cut back on. The dust is an inch thick on those bucks' antlers on the wall." She looked above her to the rafters. "I hate to think the last time this place was clean. Probably when I climbed up there and did it myself ten years ago. It's no wonder people aren't flocking here like they used to. The neighboring resorts are doing much better."

"There were skiers out there today," Jett said. "Many not too happy when we sent them home."

She sighed and dropped her head back on the craftsman chair. "Pop must be so angry. They probably all went to Taos, and he'll never see them again."

Jett took purposeful steps closer. "We had no other choice, not with a killer on this side of the mountain. I'm sure your father understands this, especially since you could have bled out because of this guy."

She stared at the fire. "I keep forgetting you don't remember anything about our time together. Pop checked out emotionally from me when Mom died twenty years ago. I've been back here for two days, and I've seen him twice in passing. He's been avoiding me. Nothing new there." She lifted her head. "He has a girlfriend. Do you know anything her?"

"Not too much. Only that Les seems happier than I've ever seen him."

She huffed and sneered. "If you're implying that I caused him to be so morose, I will have to disagree with you. He was like that long before I left." She waved her hand as though to dismiss him. "But that's right, you wouldn't know that. Only the Jett who was there for me would know all about his depression."

Jett shifted on his feet. The direction of this

conversation was going to a place he didn't want to.

"I just meant it's been a long time since you've been back. Les has been running the place solo for years. That is until Dahlia came into his life. She's been a big help to him. That's all."

"Interesting." She stared back into the fire.

"Look, Nic, we need to talk about your role here. Tomorrow morning, I will head the team up the mountain to continue the search."

"I'll be there."

"I don't think that's a good idea. You're compromised."

Anger flared from her eyes. "So I froze up a bit. I'm working on it."

He eyed her raised leg. "I was talking about your leg. But since you brought it up, what I saw on that mountain was more than a little freezing up. You were paralyzed with fear. You want to explain?"

She swallowed hard, and he wondered why he had to be the one in this situation with Nic. Don should be here.

Jett's eyes sought out the chair next to hers, but he thought better of making their predicament anything but professional and remained standing. "I have a right to know if you are putting the department at risk."

"No one is at risk. It's no big deal. I'm home because I am recuperating from a GSW."

Jett's knees threatened to buckle. He might have no choice about the chair. He glanced at her arms and shoulders, wondering where the bullet had entered.

"The back," she said as though reading his mind. "Straight through my left lung."

"On duty?"

She nodded. "Undercover. I was guarding an old man in his home. I turned my back to wash a few dishes to help, and bam! That will teach me to leave the domestic stuff to the caregiving types." Her attempt to make light of the situation fell flat.

"And your charge?"

Nic smiled sadly. "I let him down that day. He was kidnapped as I nearly died on the kitchen floor. Later, he was found safe, but not from anything I did."

"Don't you think you're being too hard on yourself? I mean, what could you have done differently?"

She looked at him. "Never turn your back. You taught me that."

The fire's crackling filled the tense silence between them as Jett struggled to respond. He had no recollection of ever teaching her anything. How could he when he had no memory of working with her. The only memories he had of her were after he woke up in the hospital. The last thing he said to her was there wouldn't be any wedding. Ever. He cringed at how he had handled the breakup, but what else could he have done? He couldn't marry someone he didn't know, never mind love.

He cleared his throat. "Look, Nic, this isn't how I would have wanted to reconnect with you. But it is, and I have a job to do, and that is to keep you safe until we find this guy. I'm sorry to hear about your gunshot. Maybe someday you can tell me more about it."

They both knew it was an empty offer. What would be the point?

"It's a nice thought, but I'm working hard to forget and move on."

Jett understood that plan of attack more than she knew. "Moving on is harder than you think."

"I've noticed." She stared into the fire. The flames shone in her green eyes, which began to shimmer with growing tears. But as fast as they came, she pressed them aside with a swipe of her slender fingers.

She placed the same hand on the armrest of the wooden chair. It was her left hand. No ring encircled her ring finger.

A quick flash blinded him with a sparkling square-cut diamond.

He blinked and looked again.

No ring.

"As for keeping me safe," Nic continued, interrupting his perplexity, "I really don't need the shadow. The sheriff has a small department. There's no reason to give Trevor up when you all need manpower. In fact, count me in to help."

Jett shook his head, in response both to her comment and to clear the image of the ring from his mind. "That won't be necessary. For one, you have a knife wound to heal from, and two, you've seen this guy's face. You can ID him. As my sole witness, I need you protected."

"All the more reason for me to help in the investigation." He watched her as she straightened in her chair, not even wincing at shifting her leg. It had to hurt her, but she didn't let on. "The perp can't hide from me. I'm helping." Her tone left no room for negotiation.

Good thing he never negotiated. "No."

With that, he turned and walked over to the dark wood check-in counter. The post was empty, and Jett contemplated ringing the small schoolhouse bell in front of him. The office door on the other side stood ajar, a light beaming brightly inside. "Les? Are you there?"

The door swung wide, but it wasn't Les.

"Hey there, Jett. Crazy day out there." Dahlia joined him at the counter. Les's girl-friend chortled, but the solemnity on her fifty-year-old face expressed the gravity of the situation. "I'm sorry to hear about the pilot, but Les sure doesn't need this right now. Shutting down the ski resort at Christmas-time could sink him. Are you sure we can't stay open? I'm working the books right now, and I have to ask if there is another way."

Jett knew the resort hadn't been doing well financially, but he hadn't realized it was on the brink of closing down. "It was Sheriff Stewart's call, but I'm hoping we will track the shooter down tomorrow, and Les can re-open right away. I would say no skiing near the crash site as that is still a crime scene."

"Do you really think the guy is still on the mountain?"

"None of the officers noticed the man come down to the base. There's a possibility he bled out in the woods along the way. If so, Tank may be able to find him, as long as the storm coming in holds off and doesn't bury him."

Dahlia scrunched her nose. "What a horrid

thing for one of the skiers to find this spring, wouldn't you say, Nic?"

Jett turned around to find Nic standing behind him. "You shouldn't be on that leg," he said.

"Let me be the judge of that." She moved up to the counter and leaned on it a bit. "I know the direction the guy was moving. It wasn't down the mountain. It was across."

"I thought you were knocked unconscious," Jett said.

"I was, but I can remember vaguely seeing him limp away before I did."

"Vaguely? I'm going to need more to go by than that." Jett wondered if she was lying just to tag along.

"Well, at this point, it's all you have. *I* am all you have. Whether you want to admit this or not, you need me." Her pursed lips and defiant eyes confirmed his apprehension about involving her.

"It doesn't matter what I need. You have already been told why your helping in this investigation is out of the question. None of that has changed in the five minutes since we talked."

Her head angled with a brazen jut to her chin. "A few stiches for a cut don't mean anything. And me being an eyewitness only helps your investigation more. Why are you so dead set against this?"

"Easy. This is not your jurisdiction. You chose the federal route and not small-town USA."

Nic's pale skin blotched, nearly matching her braided red hair. "I chose? Funny, I don't remember it quite that way. As I recall, I didn't have a choice, because you made it for me when you said there wasn't room enough in the department for both of us. And to think you didn't return anyway. Why did you boot me out?"

Had he really said that? Jett couldn't remember those words coming from him.

Trevor walked in with two steaming cups of hot cocoa. He stopped short when he felt the tension.

"I thought I told you not to let her out of your sight," Jett demanded of the deputy.

Trevor looked to Dahlia. "Les was here. I didn't think I would be that long."

"Where is he now?" Jett asked.

Dahlia replied, "Les was upset and needed some time. He said he was going for a walk. The man is really stressed out. I'm worried about his mental health."

Trouble stirred in Jett. "So stressed that he put his life at risk by going out there with a shooter on the loose? Has he been here all day? Is there anyone who can vouch for him? Any employee or guest?"

Nic's eyes rounded to saucers. "Why do I get the feeling those are interrogation questions?"

"Because they are. This is Les's mountain, and I have a lot of questions about what went down on it today. Perhaps the answers lie with you, and you don't realize it. Just how much do you know about your father's business dealings?"

The door opened and in stepped Sheriff Stewart.

"My father had nothing to do with that helicopter," Nic said.

The sheriff stomped the snow from his boots. "Actually, you'd be wrong about that, Nic. I just got the response about the tail number. That helicopter belonged to Les. Is he around? I'd like to ask him a few questions."

FIVE

Back in her chair by the fire, Nic stared into a flame that should have brought warmth and comfort but was overridden by the chaos around her. Two neighboring departments had sent a few officers over earlier that day to help with the search, and with the search on pause until morning, the police had all converged on the lobby to warm up and plan their next steps. She had been escorted back to her chair, but now with her father being targeted as a person of interest, Nic had to get in on this investigation.

She looked up at the large clock above the check-in counter. Her father had been gone for over two hours. With every second of his absence, he looked more and more suspect in what had gone down today.

Nic heard heels clicking on the wood floors behind her. She knew who was coming without having to turn her head. Pop having a girlfriend was something Nic had to get used to. A lot had changed in ten years, but Nic couldn't fault her father for wanting a companion. And Dahlia was sweet enough, she supposed.

"I'm going to start decorating the Christmas tree. It could help pass the time. Do you want to help? You can sit in the chair and hand me ornaments. It will be good for you while you wait for your dad to return." Dahlia's demeanor was upbeat and positive. She wore her bleached blond hair in a long ponytail. A pair of hooped earrings flashed, but they were nothing too gaudy. She was ten years Pop's junior, but her energetic personality might be what her father needed.

"If you don't mind, I would much rather see his accounting books."

Dahlia looked to the counter. Her drawn-on brows creased. "Why do you want to see those? This is Christmastime. Those will just depress you."

"Why didn't he tell me things were this bad for him?"

"Oh, honey, you know your dad. He keeps things bottled up. Been that way since the day we met. I'm sure a lot longer for you." Dahlia took the seat beside her.

"How did you meet?" Nic had returned to

New Mexico only two days ago and learned of her father's relationship with a woman other than his wife, Nic's mother. As long as Nic could remember, there had never been another woman for him. Claire Harrington had been everything to him until the day she'd died. Nic had never seen her father smile since that day.

Not even at her.

Dahlia stared up to the treetop on the other side of the lobby and sighed. "He was so sweet to help me. I attempted a hike up here during the summer and sprained my ankle. I thought I was a goner and would have to sleep out under the stars, I prayed no animal would get me during the night. Your dad was out on one of his walks, just like tonight. I was so blessed that he happened upon me and helped me limp all the way back down the mountain. He stayed with me until my friend could come get me... I was just tickled when he called and asked me to dinner." Dahlia wore a sweet smile as she stared into the fire. "It feels like I've known him forever. Have you ever felt like that about someone?" She looked at Nic.

Nic shot a quick glance over at Jett, remembering a time she would have been able to say yes. "I used to, but I've learned you can never really know someone completely."

"Sounds like your job has hardened you to the possibilities of love."

Nic shook her head. "Actually, my job is everything to me. It's dependable and exciting, but most of all, inclusive. The FBI is my family."

Stating this fact showed Nic why it hurt so much to be put on leave, when all she wanted was to be back at her desk or working undercover with her team. If only she could prove to her supervisor that she was ready to return. But after her unsatisfactory display on the mountain, Nic had her doubts, too.

Another reason to get in on the investigation. It could be what she needed to bounce back completely and return to her FBI fold.

"FBI. I didn't realize you were a fed. Les never told me that. How intriguing." Dahlia leaned forward and patted Nic's knee. "I'm glad you have people that care about you in your life. Being with your dad these last couple of months has been wonderful. I hope we can be friends."

Nic offered a simple smile to this woman in her father's life. Dahlia knew more about the man at this point than she did. Leaving her dad ten years ago hadn't really hurt because he had already left her ten years before that. He'd never bounced back from losing his wife.

Until Dahlia.

"I know we've just met, but if you've been able to bring joy back into Pop's life then you have done what I couldn't, and I appreciate it."

"Oh, honey, he brings me just as much joy." Dahlia stood. "I'll be over at the tree if you want to join me. There are so many people in here, I just want to get out of their way."

Listening to the plans being formed around her, Nic felt useless in her chair by the fire. The strategic special agent in her wanted to get up and be involved where it counted. Hanging decorations was fine for Dahlia, but not for Nic.

Sheriff Stewart stood by the counter with an open map of the mountain on it. "Tomorrow morning at 6:00 a.m., each team will head out with their orders. With his gunshot wound and loss of blood, this guy is probably dead, so it might be a recovery operation. Either way we must find him."

The door opened, letting a whoosh of cold air inside. Les Harrington paused in the doorway at the sight before him. "I take it you all didn't find him?"

Sheriff Stewart turned to face Nic's father. "Enjoy your walk, Les?"

"It was needed," Les responded.

"Terribly cold out there for a stroll," the sheriff said.

"I've lived on this mountain my whole life. I could survive the night if I had to. I could survive a week even." Les slowly removed his coat, laid it across the top of the check-in counter then turned back to the group. "Well, since you all will be hanging around for the night, I can have food brought in. I think I might have some cheese and crackers. Plenty of coffee, for sure." He rubbed his chin in a nervous way and kept his gaze off anyone in particular.

He knows he's under suspicion. Nic thrust herself up from the chair. She winced a bit but reined in the leg pain before anyone noticed. With all eyes on her father, it was easy to do.

Did everyone believe he was involved in this? She wasn't close with her father, but she didn't think it was possible.

Dahlia stepped away from the tree. She approached Les and said, "I'll go help you get some food together." She told everyone they'd return with some delicious munchies. "We'll be back lickety-split." She took Les's hand and led him from the room.

Les walked by Nic without even a glance. If he noticed she was in the room, he didn't let on. Then again, he rarely did. To say their relationship was strained would be an understatement. Her dad had kept to himself while she'd lived here during her teen years. Yet even though their communication was minimal, Nic still cared about her father. To see him treated as a suspect in this crime felt wrong in some way. Nic had no idea why his helicopter had been used, but there had to be a valid explanation.

Les and Dahlia disappeared up the wide staircase that led to the restaurant. As soon as they turned the corner above, Nic approached Sheriff Stewart and the group he was talking to. Jett was among them. He may have turned down her offer to assist, but Sheriff Stewart wouldn't.

Nic was sure about that.

"I want to help," Nic said, looking straight at the sheriff. "This is my mountain. I may not live here any longer, but it still belongs to me. If someone is using the resort for disreputable purposes, I have a right to know. I have a right to stop it."

Jett spoke up. "Nic, we already talked about this."

"I wasn't speaking to you," she said. Her

eyes stayed on Sheriff Stewart. "Consider the debt paid."

Jett looked between them and asked, "What debt? What are you talking about?"

Sheriff Stewart cleared his throat and put up a hand to stop Jett. "It's nothing, son. Nic and I go way back to when she was one of my deputies. She was a good cop, and I'm sure she is a great federal agent. We could use your help, Nic. That's a nice offer." He looked to her leg. "But are you sure you can cover the terrain? It's a big mountain out there."

"I've suffered worse."

Nic felt Jett's eyes on her. She had alluded to her GSW earlier, so he knew what she was talking about. Thankfully, she hadn't told him she was currently on forced leave from the Bureau. She didn't doubt that he would use it against her if he found out.

Nic looked at the group of law enforcement in front of her. "First thing we need to get clear. My father had nothing to do with this crime or criminal."

"You know we have to look at all possibilities," Sheriff Stewart said.

"Then I will have to prove you all wrong."

Jett clicked his pen and opened his notebook. He didn't like Nic being a part of the search, but she could offer eyewitness details. From his place behind the investigation teams, he listened to her describe the shooter and prepared to take notes with everyone else.

She stood by the counter, not leaning on it like before. If she was hurting, she didn't let on. Her power stance was admirable. He could tell she was used to taking charge.

"Full head of white hair, but he wasn't more than fifty years old. Not a strong build. More wiry than brawn." She tapped her thigh lightly. "I may have been injured, and he did shoot a guy, but I don't think he's the muscle behind the operation. Perhaps not even the brains. He's fairly weak without his gun. Not the streetfighter type."

"And you're positive he did not go down the mountain?" Trevor asked.

Nic shook her head. "He clutched that bag of cash tightly and limped away, heading west, toward the rim. Now, if he took a turn later and came down a different way, that is possible. But I think searching the resort is wasted. If I was leading this operation, I would look in the area of the rim."

"But you're not," Jett mumbled loud enough for the people in front of him to hear. A few turned their heads.

Stan Lieber from the Taos Police Department smirked. "Just like old times, I see." He faced forward before Jett could comprehend the investigator's words.

Nic's voice clouded Jett's thoughts. The temperature of the room felt like it had risen ten degrees. What did Stan mean by old times? Jett could only assume he referenced before the accident. What was old times to everyone else meant nothing to him.

"I'm thinking he had someone waiting for the cash." Nic's answer to someone's question pulled his attention back to her. "I do not think he was working alone. Any other questions?"

A hand rose up front. "Not a question, Nic, but just a welcome back. Nice to see you haven't changed a bit."

Jett took the comment as a slight against him. He's the only one who had changed. He knew people talked about him, but up until this moment, he hadn't let it bother him. He never wanted anyone's pity, but he did want people to stop expecting him to know them, and even to know his job in the department. He'd worked hard since the moment he woke up in the hospital after being in a coma for over a month. People came and went from his room with no recollection, until they stopped coming. After two years of not regaining his memories, and his duties as a deputy, he had given up his badge. Changing over to Search and Rescue was the better fit for him anyways. But perhaps all this time the other law enforcement had wished it had been Nic who'd stayed on instead. Maybe that's the real reason they talked about him. He had made her leave.

Trevor walked up to Jett and whispered, "Does this mean I'm off the hook babysitting her?"

Jett nearly released him from the duty, but then remembered how he'd felt when he'd come upon all that blood on the mountainside. The woman may be able to do her job well, but that didn't negate the fact that someone wanted her dead. "Stay on her."

"Any reason why? Seems like overkill to me. The lady knows what she's doing." Trevor spoke under his breath as he watched her address the group, even giving orders. And Sheriff Stewart was letting her.

That was a whole other area to look into. Jett would love to know what debt she'd been talking about that the sheriff owed her. Whatever it was, it had put her at the front of the line.

Les and Dahlia descended the staircase carrying trays of food and drinks. They placed the trays on the oversized coffee tables around the room. The group dispersed to partake in the snacks.

Jett had no desire to eat anything. The only thing on his mind was hearing a solid answer from Les about why his helicopter had been used by the shooter. He took the moment to approach Les to get some answers.

"Hey, Les, I have some questions about the helicopter crash. I know I'm not a deputy, but perhaps you can help me understand how this happened at Wild Mountain. Would you mind?"

Dahlia excused herself. "I'll just be over at the tree, hanging some ornaments. Nic, you mind helping with the garland?"

Nic looked between Jett and her father. Jett could tell she wanted to say no, but when she looked to her father, he said without looking at her, "Go help her decorate."

Jett couldn't help but notice that the bravado Nic had only moments before displayed in front of the teams evaporated at her father's dismissal. Their strained relationship would explain why she had stayed away for so long. Jett had no right to say anything about Nic's family situation. Not when his own was just as broken. He'd skipped the family Thanksgiving this year, and Christmas wasn't looking too good, either.

As Dahlia held the garland up, she walked around the tree in full sight of the window beside it. Nic kept herself out of the view. He was glad to see she had smarts. Maybe she didn't need a tail after all.

Jett gave Les his full attention and asked the question that had been plaguing him. "We all know things are financially tight for you right now. We assume you rented out your helicopter to this man. Can you tell us anything about him and why you did this?"

Les shrugged and waved his hands in front of him. "I told the sheriff I had nothing to do with the rental. The chopper was for sale. People over at the airfield are handling all that for me. The last message I received was to let me know someone rented it for a weekend getaway two weeks ago. But if this guy told the airfield that he wanted to test run it for possible purchase, I wouldn't be called. I wish I could help more." He looked at the tables of food. "This is all I really can do for you. I hope I don't have to remain closed for much longer. This could put me under."

Glass shattered across the room.

Jett jumped, only to realize it was a glass bulb.

"I am so clumsy tonight," Dahlia said,

moving to pick up the pieces. "Ouch." She put her finger in her mouth; she obviously cut herself on a piece of glass.

Nic walked around the tree. "Here, let me see how bad it is."

Dahlia waved her away. "Nonsense, honey. It's just a little cut." She bent to pick up the shards. Jett realized Nic was now standing in front of the window. He started to walk slowly toward her, knowing she was exposed and at risk.

With each step, more concern grew. The hair on the back of his neck stood, but his feet wouldn't move fast enough. The next seconds felt like an eternity.

"Nic, move!" His order sounded like an order for Tank.

Tank heard him loud and clear and jumped up from his spot by the door. "Tank." Jett whistled and his K-9 lurched forward. A wave of his arm at Nic with the order, "Down."

She squinted in confusion as Tank went barreling at her. She raised her hands as Jett circled the table, jostling through a group of officers talking. He ignored their complaints.

Tank pushed up on his hindlegs and pro-jected himself through the air while Jett ap-proached her in his own dive by her legs.

Nic screamed as she went down at the same

moment that Jett landed on the ground with a thud. The window blasted inward just as he had feared. He twisted around to cushion Nic's fall as she came down, and all three of them slid across the wood floor in a heap.

Commotion ensued as the sheriff belted out orders and lawmen went into full operation mode. Jett moved Nic down to the floor and flung an arm around her until he could process the scene. Only a crying Dahlia, Les Harrington and Sheriff Stewart remained in the room.

When he started to move away from Nic, her knuckled grip on his shirt wouldn't let him. He looked down into her face, their noses inches from each other. Her green eyes were wide pools of fear. Her paled lips were trembling.

"Was I hit?" she breathed and swallowed hard.

Jett looked behind him to the wooden beam by the counter and could see where it had splintered. He shook his head and took in her fearful expression. Her slender fingers held on to him for dear life. "I knocked you over in time, but I won't say you're all right." He covered her hand with one of his and tried to remove her hold.

"Please don't tell the sheriff," she whispered. "I'm working through it." Deep, steady breaths came from her.

Jett glanced over to the sheriff, who was taking Dahlia and Les into the safety of the office. "You belong with your father," Jett said.

She shook her head, let go and pushed him away. She scuttled backward and sat upright. Reaching into her waistband behind her, she pulled out her gun. "I belong out there."

Jett couldn't let her run out into the dark, not with a bull's-eye on her back. "Fine, I won't say anything about your fear to the sheriff. This time. But you must know you are too rattled to go out there tonight. Stay low and get yourself ready for tomorrow."

Thankfully, she saw reason, but she kept her gun on her leg for the remainder of the evening.

SIX

"Do you have to follow me wherever I go?" Nic asked Trevor the following morning. Teams were already dispersing to their mountain locations to start searching for the shooter. Nic put on a pair of gloves before heading out into the bitter morning cold.

"Sorry, I'm not to let you out of my sight. Jett's orders. You're the only one who can ID this guy. That makes you our new best friend. I'm to stick to you like glue."

She glanced in the direction Jett and Tank had gone. She no longer could see them through the trees, just the two sets of tracks they'd left behind. "He is so different now."

Trevor frowned. "Don't mind him. It's nothing personal. He always works alone. It's amazing he even radioed for backup yesterday. I've never heard him so concerned as when he saw all that blood up there. If I didn't know better, I would have thought he remembered you. He was in frenzy to find you. Jett was actually scared at what we would find. Can you believe it? Jett, scared? That man doesn't feel fear. He doesn't feel anything. He's like a robot going through his day." Trevor shook his head. "But yesterday on this mountain, that guy was shaking in his boots."

Nic frowned. "It wasn't one of my best moments. I'm sorry I lost the guy and put you all through that."

Trevor shrugged and started up the mountain.

"Are you sure he doesn't remember anything? I mean I know he didn't after the accident, but have any memories come back to him over the years?" She looked to Trevor to gauge his response to her questions.

"If they have, he hasn't shared anything with us. And probably not his family, either."

"Not even his parents?" Nic found this hard to believe. Jett had always been close to his parents and siblings. "What about his younger brother? He and Truman had been inseparable." Nic thought of the years she'd spent with the two brothers mapping the mountain on their scouting endeavors on foot and snowmobile.

"I'm sad to say the Butler family pretty

much fragmented after the accident. They couldn't handle being around him. Mister and missus moved to Santa Fe. His sister, Luci, went to Albuquerque. And Tru went to Carlsbad. He's a guide there now. Jett took the house and lives there alone."

Nic was shocked to hear how the accident had destroyed Jett's family. "Did he push them away like he pushed me?"

"Pretty much, but you didn't hear it from me. He got tired pretending he remembered any of them. They got tired of being reminded that he didn't."

"Sounds discouraging on all sides. I'm sorry to hear things went south for them after I left. I had hoped he would remember them at least." Nic sighed and climbed onto the back of the snowmobile she and Trevor would share for the day. Her leg ached, but she hoped the cold would numb it soon. She took up the helmet, placed it over her head and strapped it on tight.

Before lowering the face shield, she said, "So many times I've wished I could go back to that night and yank that wheel when I saw the truck coming. It was like I couldn't believe the guy was going to run the red light. My doubt ruined everything."

Trevor secured his helmet and climbed onto

the front portion of the snowmobile seat. He shouted over his shoulder, "The hit and run ruined everything." With that, he started the engine and put it into gear.

The screaming noise of the snowmobile's engine cut into Nic's memories of that night. Except there hadn't been any screeching of either vehicle's brakes. Jett'd had the green light. The truck had never slowed down.

Nic closed her eyes as they ascended the mountain. The mangled crunching of the crashing vehicles was just as loud in her mind now as it had been ten years ago. But no matter how significant that moment had been in her life, she knew that, for Jett, it had been a pivotal moment that divided his life into two separate parts: before the accident and after.

And now to learn that his family had been destroyed because of it, as well, Nic wondered if she could let her own pain of being forgotten go. Could she except this new Jett and treat him as any other person she met?

So many hopes and dreams, not to mention the sweet kisses they'd shared would have to be locked away forever, as if they'd never happened. The thought sent a shiver through her. It made her wonder if she had ever fully let go of him.

Trevor brought them to the location they were to search and killed the motor. She had made sure she'd assigned herself to the elevation at the midway point. It was a place just a bit higher than where she'd last seen the suspect hobble off.

"You really think this guy went back up the mountain and not down?" Trevor asked as he stood. "I'm having my doubts of finding anything this far up."

Nic remained seated as she surveyed the terrain around them. The untouched snow shone like glass in the sunrise coming over the peaks. She looked down the slope to where the only disturbance of the snow had been made by the snowmobile's ski tracks. She looked behind her into the trees and thought of where she had been knocked unconscious.

"I figure I was about a hundred feet across and down from here. If he didn't head over this slope here, then he either went down to the base or—"

"Don't say it," Trevor warned.

She didn't comply. "He went farther up."

"Why would he go up if he was hurt?"

"Because he had someone waiting for him." Nic pointed to the seat in front of her. "Get back on. We go higher."

"Fine, but I have to inform the teams we are moving up our location." Trevor radioed their change in location.

Ten seconds later, Jett's voice charged through the speaker. "That is not the plan that was made. Do not change course. I repeat, do not change course. I will come up there and remove you from the search if I have to."

Nic reached for her own radio at her belt. "We're going up another hundred yards. If I don't see any signs of someone crossing over, I will say he went down." She turned the radio off and said to Trevor, "Move out before he comes up here."

Trevor shook his head and climbed back on the snowmobile. "Remind me to never get on your bad side."

"What's that supposed to mean?" she asked, but he'd started the engine and drowned her out.

Minutes later and eighty yards higher, a disruption in the snow's surface caught Nic's eye. She tapped Trevor on the shoulder and pointed forward. The nod of his helmet told her he saw it, too.

He drove the snowmobile up to the spot and stopped. They lifted their visors and stared at the unmistakable tracks of human boot prints.

Blood smeared along the way.

"Never mind what I said. I won't doubt you again." Trevor reached for his radio. "Tracks found," he announced to the teams, and gave their coordinates.

Once again, Jett broke in. "Stay put. I'm coming up."

Trevor looked at Nic.

Nic shook her head. "Time's wasting. Let's move." They removed their helmets and left them on the seat. As she climbed off and headed for the trees, she thought perhaps treating Jett like one of the guys wouldn't be so hard after all.

Trevor informed the others of their plans to search the woods. Jett's angered voice could be heard behind her. She was glad she had turned the volume on her radio down.

"He's not happy about this," Trevor said as he caught up.

Nic reached the first row of the trees, staying back from the tracks so they would be preserved. As she studied where they led, she mused aloud, "I find this interesting."

"The tracks?"

"No, the fact that I'm trying to forget Jett because he doesn't remember me, and yet he claims to not remember me and can't seem to get me out of his mind."

* * *

"Come on, Tank." Jett climbed onto his snowmobile while his dog jumped into the enclosed case mounted to the rear seat. "That woman is going to walk straight into trouble again."

Thoughts of the night before with the window shattering around her plagued him. His gut had told him moments before that danger followed her, just as it told him so now. She may think she's doing the tracking, but she could be walking right into a trap.

He made haste and careened up the mountain until he could see the snowmobiles by the trees. Mac and his team of three had already arrived. Jett pulled to a stop and jumped off. Tank followed in one great leap from his box, swishing his tail and ready for the hunt.

"The guy definitely came through here," Mac told him. The tracks with smears of blood proved the injured man had made it this far.

Jett peered into the trees to follow the evidence. "He couldn't have stayed up here if he shot through the window last night."

At Nic.

Jett's stomach churned.

Mac cut into Jett's horrific memory. "What other way down could he have used? The gorge on the other side of those trees drops off. He would have had to go farther up and around, and with this much blood loss, I don't see him surviving that hike through the snow."

Jett had to agree. "Then Nic was right. Our shooter was meeting someone."

Mac smiled. "She was always right about things. Smart and brave, that one."

Jett shook his head. "Was she always so impulsive?"

Mac huffed. "Some might say courageous, but that's just me, I suppose."

"Some might, but not me. Order is what is needed to succeed. I can't have her running off every time she gets a whiff of a clue. Even Tank knows not to chase every scent."

The K-9 sat back on his haunches and whined, lifting a paw as though to say *I'm ready.*

"Move out," Jett told Tank.

Following his dog through the woods, he soon picked up Nic and Trevor's tracks. When he came out on the other side of the trees, he found Trevor standing at the edge of the gorge. Nic was nowhere in sight.

"Where is she?" Jett demanded.

Trevor pointed down, and Jett grunted in dissatisfaction. He shouldn't be surprised she would put her life in jeopardy again. "Why would she climb down there? It is obvious by the ski tracks that this guy had a ride down the mountain from here."

"Not before he stashed something down here. Or lost it," Nic announced from somewhere below.

Just as Jett reached the edge, Nic's head popped up.

In her gloved hand, she waved a plastic evidence bag. Inside it, a red knit cap. She continued, "I'm sure we'll find DNA on this. The wind was blowing yesterday. I wonder if he even realized this blew off as he was dashing down the mountain."

Jett could tell Nic was quite proud of her find. He looked past her into the gorge and saw where she had climbed down to a skinny ledge to retrieve the cap.

"Have you always been this reckless?"

"You mean do I go after what I want and get it?" She smirked. "No matter the cost."

"Even at the expense of life and limb. What if you had fallen? Did you not think about the rest of the teams? How you would have put their lives in jeopardy to go after you?"

"I know the risks. If I didn't think I could make it down and back, I wouldn't have done it." She lifted the cap to him. "Take the evidence bag. I don't want one hair falling out of it. You think you can handle getting it to the lab? Or should I take care of that myself, too?"

Jett didn't reach for the bag. When Trevor realized he wasn't going to, the deputy took it from her instead.

Nic moved to raise a leg and boost herself up over the ledge. Instantly, she cried out in pain. "I think I just popped a stitch."

Begrudgingly, Jett knelt to give her a hand up, but the sound of ice cracking halted him. In the next second, Nic lost her ledge hold. A quick move only allowed him to grab the back of her coat. Just a few fibers lay between his fingertips. He sank into the snow and started to slip toward the edge.

Nic screamed as she grasped at the rocky ledge.

"Hold on! I got you!" Jett said the words but knew he really didn't have a secure grip. "Try not to move!" He slipped closer to the edge, losing his balance as the heavier weight was on the wrong side. She would take him down with her. "Trevor, grab my legs," he shouted. "But if we slip, let go. You understand me?"

"I'm not letting you guys go!" Trevor's voice strained with the effort of holding the weight of two people.

Jett locked his gaze on Nic's. Stark fear shone up at him as she tried to remain still. "Swing your right arm around and grab hold of my arm," he instructed her.

"What if my movement makes you lose your grip?"

"Then we both go down. Trevor will let go." Jett was very calm as he spoke. That would be the plan. "I'm not letting go. So do as I say. Swing your arm around and grab hold of my arm."

Nic angled her head to look up at him. He could see the doubt in her eyes. She had no reason to trust him. She had no reason to believe that he would hold on. When he woke up from his coma, he had pushed her away and cut her out of his life.

What had he feared, he wondered?

Suddenly, as he stared down into her fierce green eyes, Jett knew those eyes had the power to see into his past, where he only saw darkness.

If he let her go now, he would never learn what had happened the night of the accident. Up until this moment, he hadn't realized he really wanted to know.

Jett tightened his grip. Rescuing Nic could be his most important rescue in his career.

"Now, Nic," he said, giving a single nod of assurance for her to make her move.

For the briefest of moments, she closed her eyes and took a deep breath. The next second, with all her might, she twisted her body and swung her arm up full-force.

The snow ledge beneath Jett shifted again as he twisted his body in an attempt to pull her up and over him. Or out and over the gorge, if he'd miscalculated.

He heard the crack of breaking ice before he felt the ground beneath him dislodge. He had no time to shout as Nic's weight pulled him down headfirst. The ground gave way and the two of them dropped from the ledge.

SEVEN

Nic dropped a foot, then jolted to a stop. She stared up into Jett's horrified eyes then took a quick scan of her situation. She'd managed to grab hold of his forearm as planned. He still had the back of her coat locked in his grip.

"Hang on!" Trevor could be heard from above them. How could he pull them both up? All she could do was hang on. Her total trust was in these two men, but was that foolish of her? These were not men who'd fought for her before. Their previous decisions had been to push her away.

"Please, Jett…" she said through a breathless rasp, not even sure what she wanted to ask. Begging for anything from this man had been fruitless in the past. Sweat burst from his forehead as he strained to hold her. She knew he couldn't hold on much longer. She knew Trevor could not pull them both up. "I forgive you," she said. "It's okay."

Nic not only spoke for this moment, but her forgiveness covered all past offenses. She knew she had to let go. She did not want him to spend the rest of his life feeling guilty.

A strained moan escaped his lips as he attempted to hold her up. "Letting go is never okay. I won't…let…go."

A growling from above cut into the thunder of the blood pumping through her mind. Her own whimpers of fright mixed with Tank's grunts. She could only assume he was holding on to Jett in some way, and would hold on to the death.

"You have to. Tank will go off this ledge with you, if you don't," Nic implored him. "I'm not afraid to die."

"I've noticed," Jett said and gave a loud, labored shout as he lifted her to follow him over the edge.

Suddenly, Nic found herself lying flat on the snow. Her legs dangled off the ledge, but Jett gave one more pull until she was fully on solid ground.

He fell onto his back, while she fought for breath in the realization that she was safe. Tank's cold nose sniffed her cheek, but Nic could only lift a hand to touch his fur. All her energy had been used in holding on for dear life.

"Do me a favor…" Jett breathed rapidly from beside her.

"What?" She spoke the word but wasn't sure it even came out clearly.

"Stop putting yourself in danger."

Nic lifted her head slightly. "That's not how this works, and you know it. We are the ones who head into danger when everyone else runs the other way. You could have let me go."

Jett shook his head. "That's not how I do my job. I am Search and Rescue."

Nic laid her face into the snow. She heard the running of more officers as they came running through the woods toward them. "Now the cavalry shows up."

"You didn't have to climb down to get the hat." Jett rubbed his face and sat up.

"Would you have let me if you had known?"

Jett laughed. "Not on your life."

Nic smirked at him. "Then it was worth it." She pushed up on her arms and looked out over the drop into the gorge. "But I thank you for coming to my rescue." She eyed him just as the officers arrived. "I meant what I said before."

Jett's smile fell from his face. He gave a single nod. "Thank you. I didn't know I needed it until you said it."

The strained moment between them quickly turned to chaotic order as the search teams took over to care for them. Nic felt herself being lifted and checked even as she said she was fine. The group separated, and Nic looked up to see her former boss coming her way. She braced herself for his displeasure.

Sheriff Stewart knelt by her side. "You all right?"

Nic gave a quick nod. "Jett rescued me when the ledge gave out." She glanced at Trevor. "You have the hat?"

The deputy reached into his coat pocket and took out the plastic evidence bag containing the red knit cap. He nodded. "We got it. Or I should say, you got it."

Nic looked back at the sheriff. "I only attempted it because I was sure I could get it."

Stewart frowned and shook his head. "You were always one to go after what you wanted. I always knew that you would land on your feet. It's why I was tough on you." He leaned in close. "But next time, ask for help. We're a team here. You have nothing to prove with us."

As the sheriff stood to give the teams their next orders, including getting the hat to forensics for analysis, Nic straightened beside Tank and let the sheriff's words wash over her. Nothing to prove. How had he known that's all she knew how to do? Her whole life was about proving her place.

"Now get a move on, everyone! Our shooter is no longer up here," Sheriff Stewart instructed. "The snow has started. The storm is here. It is time to get off this mountain."

Nic looked up to find snowflakes falling from the sky. She wondered when it had started and how she had missed it. In her focus to prove herself, she'd missed the urgency of the storm.

As the search teams dispersed, Nic realized Jett had stayed sitting beside her. His dog stoically stood guard between them.

"Why do you call him Tank? He's not that big." She reached out and petted where the black fur of the husky met the white fur right below his ears.

"He's not called that because of his size." Jett shifted and straightened his left leg. His blue snow leggings, shredded at the calf and topped with traces of blood, looked as though he'd been mauled by an animal. Before she could ask what happened, Jett said, "You're alive right now because of Tank's strength and determination, and a bit of his stubbornness. When he digs in his heels about something, he's not messing around. He locked his legs up and held on to my leg with his teeth."

"He bit you to keep us from going over?" She'd seen law enforcement dogs hold down suspects but never their handlers.

"I wouldn't call it a bite. He held on the only way he could, giving Trevor time to pull us up." Jett ruffled Tank's fur behind his ears. The dog whimpered in enjoyment and opened his mouth. The sharp teeth explained the tears in Jett's leggings.

Nic eyed the precipice. The snow showed where the dog had dug in and locked his legs tight to anchor the two of them from falling.

"Strong like a tank," she mumbled. "I understand."

"Up here on these treacherous mountains, strength tops size," Jett said.

She looked back at Jett and his dog. The two were the team that she and Jett had always planned to be long before the accident. What she lacked in size, she made up for in strength. To allow herself to work with him again felt like another ledge she could go over. They both still hung from some sort of precipice, one that felt more dangerous to her. This proverbial abyss had the power to derail her from life as she knew it. Willingly letting

Jett back in would be much riskier than retrieving the killer's hat.

Could she do it?

She glanced down at his tattered ski pants and realized he already had a partner. "I'm sorry he had to do this to you because of me. If the ledge hadn't given out, I would have had no problem getting back up. Please know I don't typically make foolish choices, and I had thought this through before climbing down to get the hat."

Jett shrugged. "I would have made the same choice. But still, from now on, I need you to include me before you head into danger."

Her head snapped up. "So you can stop me? I'm a federal agent. Danger doesn't scare me."

"That is why I will be sticking close to you during this investigation," he said. "I'm not making this mistake again. Plus, you have something I need."

Nic stood and steadied her herself on wobbly knees. Strength or no, she had just almost fallen to her death. "What could I possibly have that you need?"

Jett rose and reached for her arm. When she flinched at his touch, he dropped his hand and waved her toward the path to the snowmobiles. "Memories, Nicole," he responded from behind her, words only she could hear. "I need your memories."

Heavy snow reigned the mountain all day. A foot of fresh powder had already accumulated around the base lodge.

"The crash site will be buried," Jett said, bringing Nic a cup of coffee. He placed it beside her on the long, split tree trunk now used as a desk. The knotty cut of wood was older than she was and had been in her dad's office long before he'd bought the resort. They'd always figured the room had been built around the piece. "At least Mac and Trevor were able to process it as much as possible before the storm." Jett pulled up a chair to sit and looked out the window to see the snow whipping sideways in the early evening sky.

"We have the hat," Nic reminded him, not looking up from her father's ledger. "It's only a matter of time until his DNA identifies him." She bit down on the pencil in her hand, and it snapped. Tossing it, she opened the drawer and rummaged past a flashlight and scrap paper for another one. She scribbled something on a pad of paper and underlined it with a thick, straight line of graphite.

"Only if he's got a record," Jett reminded her, leaning over to read what she wrote.

"Be careful," she warned. "You don't have a warrant to look at these ledgers."

"I'm not law enforcement."

"But you're still connected."

Jett leaned back in his chair and cleared his throat. "You want to play like that?"

"I want to play by the rules. I won't risk this guy getting off on a technicality. Lawyers would have a field day if they learned information was obtained without permission or a warrant."

"Are you sure you're not just protecting your father?"

Nic put the pencil down and faced him. "Of course I'm protecting my father. I have not kept my intentions a secret. I don't want to see him take the fall for this guy."

"He would only take the fall for his own crimes. He wasn't on that mountain and didn't kill anyone."

"But you're still searching for a way to tie him to it. Go ahead and deny it," she dared with a lift to her chin.

He couldn't. And wouldn't.

Jett shrugged. "We're searching for the reason that helicopter was up there. If that means your father has the information we need, then so be it."

Nic glanced back at the ledger and pursed

her lips. With a sigh, she said, "I'm missing a book."

Jett leaned closer again. "Do you mind if I look?" he asked this time.

She slid the open ledger toward him and flipped to the last page. "There's nothing incriminating, so why not? There's also nothing helpful here. This is the most current book I have, and its last entry is from a year ago."

Jett glanced up at the shelf above them. Rows of archived ledgers led back to at least sixty years. "Are you sure it's not mixed in with older books?"

She tapped the ledger in front of them. "This is the newest one here. I've looked in every drawer and on every shelf. I even dared to search the closet."

The floor of the packed little room off the back supported its spilled contents. "How brave of you."

"When I'm on a mission, nothing will deter me."

"So I've noticed," Jett mumbled and scanned the wood-paneled room around him, looking for any other place the ledger could have been stashed. A counter ran along one side of the room with two windows above it. A cabinet was underneath the counter. "How about under the fax machine cabinet?"

"Already looked, and no. If there is a ledger, it's not here."

"How about a computer? Maybe your dad transferred over to a spreadsheet software."

Nic laughed. "He doesn't even have an email. I can't imagine him ever changing his archaic system."

"Even with Dahlia's help?" Jett asked. "She's not old school like your father."

Nic pressed her lips together, looking like she wanted to say something but was hesitant.

"What is it?" he asked.

She shrugged and glanced out the door toward the lobby. When she turned back, she lowered her voice to a near whisper. "How long have they been dating?"

"You don't know?" The idea that Nic was so disconnected from her only parent felt odd. But then, he wasn't one to judge. His own family had dispersed to corners away from him. "Three months, I guess. Maybe four. She's been helping him around here for at least three anyway… Maybe you could ask him where the ledger is, without alerting him to why?" Jett asked.

Nic frowned. "In case you haven't noticed, my dad barely talks to me."

He'd noticed, but no words came to offer solace. It wasn't his place anyway.

Jett slapped his hands on his thighs. "Okay, so we have one missing ledger to search for." He stood, putting space between them. Breathing became easier, and he wondered why he hadn't noticed he'd been struggling in the first place.

A glimpse of Nic's profile as she returned to the ledger's last two pages had him perplexed. No recollection of their past came to mind and yet... And yet he couldn't ignore the fact that the deep feeling tightening his chest had to have come from someplace within him.

"You still do that." Her words stirred him from his thoughts.

"Do what?" he asked, nervousness setting in. Had she caught him staring? How could he explain when he didn't have an answer himself?

"Pull your earlobe when you are deep in thought," she said and mimicked his reflexive movement.

"Interesting." He let go of his ear and rubbed his fingers and thumb as his hand fell to his side. "I guess I never thought to ask if I did that before the accident. And no one ever told me...until now."

The room plummeted into a heavy, uncomfortable silence. The idea that she could have told him lots of things had he not driven her away hung between them.

"I'm going to take a look around for any other places the ledger could be kept. Maybe out in the check-in area." As he turned to leave, she stopped him with a question.

"You mentioned on the mountain that you want my memories. Did you mean things like your earlobe, or something more substantive?"

"More substantive." Without looking back, he said, "I want to know who hit me. I want to know what you remember from that night."

"I see." She took a deep breath. "It won't lead to anything."

"How do you know?"

She let the breath out slowly. "Because I already looked for him. I'm sorry to tell you, but it's a dead end."

EIGHT

The next morning, Nic agreed to go with Jett to his home in downtown Taos. He pulled his Search and Rescue utility truck into his driveway and up to the doors of his two-car garage. The house itself was a ranch-style home that was filled with so many wonderful memories for her.

"I wish your parents were here," she said without thinking. "Oh, I'm sorry."

He shrugged. "Their choice. They retired to Santa Fe."

He opened his car door, stepped out, and she followed his lead out her own side. Tank leaped from the car and gave his whole body a good shake. He ran an excited circle around Jett before racing up to the front door to wait for them.

Nic laughed. "He's eager to get inside." She stepped up the steps and patted the dog's head. Tank's striking gray-blue eyes danced at the touch.

"He knows there are snacks waiting for him."

Tank's ears perked straight up at the word snacks, causing Nic to chuckle as Jett unlocked the door and held it wide for her. Tank rushed in first.

"Hey, how about some manners?" Jett called after his dog.

"I don't blame him. Snacks are a good motivator." Nic stepped inside and inhaled deeply of the memories she had of the room before her.

The small stucco house had arched windows and doorways reminiscent of a Mexican hacienda. Tank's nails clicked over brown-tile flooring along the hall that led to the kitchen at the back of the house. The two followed the dog.

Nic noticed there were no pictures on the hallway walls like there used to be.

"What happened to all the photos?" she asked.

"For a while, I kept them up." He passed by the kitchen breakfast bar and opened the door to the garage. "I let my family take them. They meant more to them than they did to

me. What I want to show you is out here."
He held the door open.

Nic sighed and stepped forward. He wanted
her memories from the night of the accident.
He didn't want her opinion about his lack of
family photos on the wall.

"Have you ever considered that your memories might return if you surrounded yourself
with the people of your past?" She stopped in
front of him and waited for an answer. When
none came, she said, "Well?"

"Interesting you would say that. They
thought the same thing after you left."

"'Left'?"

"You know what I mean." He looked past
her shoulder to the garage behind her. Beyond the red pickup parked inside, there was
some shelving at the far end. He eyed the various haphazardly stashed boxes and tools then
looked back at her. "They forced pictures of
you on me daily."

Nic understood what he was saying. Pictures did not do the trick. "I guess that would
have been too easy." She sighed and turned to
face the garage. "All right, what do you want
to show me?"

"It's over there on the shelves." He led the
way, taking down a box on the top shelf. He
walked over and placed it on the hood of the

truck. With his hand paused on the folded flaps, he took a deep breath before giving a hard pull and opening it wide.

Nic stepped up close to peer inside and found it filled with an assorted collection of items that had no rhyme or reason. She reached in and removed a packet of envelopes grouped together by an elastic band. She looked into the box again and found an ice scraper, a first-aid kit and a wool blanket. She lifted the blanket and found an old pack of gum, unopened. There was also a smaller box with no lid. She put the envelopes on the hood of the pickup then reached into the smaller box.

"Are these your map notebooks?" she asked, flipping the top one open.

Jett moved closer and looked over. "You tell me."

Nic frowned at the gravity of the situation. "You really don't remember making these maps?"

"If I did, I wouldn't need you here." He tapped the rim of the larger box. "This is everything that was in the car from the night of the accident. The car was totaled, but they salvaged these things and boxed them up for me. They didn't mean anything to me then, and they don't now."

"Then why are you showing them to me?"

Jett shrugged. "I thought they might trigger something from that night. I mean for you, not me."

Nic flipped through the lidless box, lifting out and unfolding one notebook after the other. "These maps were hand drawn by you and Tru. You spent years traversing the mountain to get them down. You really don't remember?" She let the truth of the matter settle around her. His amnesia had destroyed every relationship in his life.

"I don't want your pity. I want your memories. That's it." His blue eyes pierced her with all seriousness.

"I understand, but I'm still sad for everyone. What happened that night was unfair."

"Is that why you looked for the guy?"

Nic was silent as she thought of her answer. "I guess that is what I told myself. But...if I'm honest, I was trying to avenge all that I'd lost."

She stopped short at admitting that that loss had included him. It was an obvious fact that didn't need to be voiced. She glanced down at the map notebook again, forcing the change in conversation.

"You and your brother loved making these. You guys would disappear for days while you surveyed the terrain. He really looked up to you and trusted your wisdom on the mountain." She turned the page and froze.

Nic felt her heartbeat pick up its pace at the map she held in her hand. It was a survey of their property they were going to live on once they were married. Jett had built their home, and it had been nearly complete before… Her breaths shallow, she forced herself to breathe deep.

"What is it?" Jett asked and leaned over. "Oh." He reached for the smaller box and put it back in the larger one. "These maps don't matter. They have nothing to do with the hit and run. This was just in the car and probably had been there for a while."

"Have you been there? To the house?"

He shrugged. "A few times. My parents took me up there after I was released from the hospital. It's been years now. It's not important."

Their home wasn't important? Was any of this stuff then? She eyed the bound stack of envelopes. "What does any of this have to do with the crash?"

"I don't know. For a while, I didn't open the box. I didn't want to know."

"Pushing it away, like you did everything

that reminded you of your life before that night. And everyone." She made her point clear.

"What if…"

She waited for him to continue while her attention zeroed in on the top letter in the stack.

"Nothing. Forget I said anything." Jett moved to grab up the envelopes, but she stopped him, placing her hand over his on the stack. "I shouldn't have brought you here. It was foolish, not to mention dangerous with this guy on the loose. I need to get you back. Consider it a lapse in judgment." His hand curled around the stack.

"Stop," she said. "Is that top one what I think it is?"

"What?" He lifted his hand for them to identify the letter. "'Taos County Clerk's Office,'" he read from the address stamped on the upper left corner. His face paled. "I'm not sure."

Nic removed the envelope from the stack and noted it had been torn open. She reached in for the letter. Unfolding it, she prepared herself for what she already knew it to be.

Their marriage license.

Her hands trembled and her vision blurred. With her breath held in her chest, she forced herself to find their names on the legal document meant to unite them as husband and wife for the rest of their lives.

She rubbed her thumb over their signatures at the bottom. "We were so excited to sign this," she said, her thoughts on the memory of that rainy day. As the horror that followed on their drive home broke into her recollections, she quickly refolded the letter and shoved it at Jett's chest. He grabbed it before it fell.

"I'll meet you out front. I don't need any of these things to help me remember that night." She reached into the box with the map notebooks and took the one of her mountain. "I will take this, though." She didn't mention how her memory of the mountain's terrain had been failing her. Perhaps the map would help her.

She skirted the hood of the truck and on her way hit the button to open the garage door. Jett's truck sat in the driveway where they had left it. Outside, she heard the garage door closing behind her and turned to see Jett pocket the letter inside his coat.

"Why are you keeping it? It's trash," she said. "Throw it away."

"Well, actually, in the State of New Mexico marriage licenses never expire. I'll see about having it voided. I apologize for bringing you here and having to see this."

"Voided. Just like you so easily voided our relationship." She crossed her arms in front of her, a way to protect herself from any more rejection from him. A car coming down the street revved its engine and she turned to see a blue sedan picking up speed.

"Get down!" Jett yelled from behind her.

The next moment a gunshot exploded through the air and glass shattered from somewhere. Breaths whooshed from Nic's lungs as she hit the ground at full force. Her face smashed against the pavement, and she felt Jett on her back. Tank's frenzied barking from inside the house matched her heart rate. Her breathing grew shallow and fast as she heard Jett hit his radio button to call in the drive-by shooting she had just survived.

Barely.

"Nic, you can get up now! We need to go after him."

She heard Jett's shouting. She felt him jostle her shoulder. She wanted to make a move, to go after the guy.

None of that mattered, because she was frozen…again. There would be no denying her problem to Jett now. She forced the words out. "J-just go on w-without me."

Jett radioed directions for one of the officers to answer the call.

Why wasn't he going? Why was he sitting beside her, rubbing her back?

"Go, Jett." She spoke with her face still planted against the cement.

"Sorry, but I don't leave my partner." He continued to rub. When her erratic breathing eased, he said, "You have no business being on duty, but I guess you already knew that." When she didn't respond, he added, "Give me one good reason why I should keep you around."

Slowly, Nic raised her head. She glared at him. "Because you owe me from the last time you didn't."

Jett drove across town to a small retirement community. Nic sat beside him in silence, while Tank stared out the window at snowy fields from the rear seat of the truck.

"How are you feeling?" he asked.

She shrugged and kept her attention out the passenger window. "What happened back there won't happen again."

"You can't be sure of that."

She faced him. "Look, I'm trying to figure it out, okay? All I know is I'm fine until a gunshot goes off. I didn't freeze up hanging off the ledge, so why does my body react this way with a gun?"

"Trauma has a way of messing with us physiologically. That's why I'm concerned about you approaching this house. If this guy is here, he could come out with guns blazing. As much as you think you can control it, you can't."

"Jett, I have to, or I'm done. I might as well give my notice and buy a farm, or something."

He held in a laugh until he saw her smirk. Then he let it go. "A farm?"

"Yeah, isn't that where our parents sent our pets when they couldn't handle life anymore?" She smiled, and he found it softened her toughness…and took his laughter away.

"I'm pretty sure you aren't finished yet. When I realized I couldn't handle being a deputy, I found another way to find purpose in life."

"But I don't want another way. I take down bad guys, and that's all I want to do." Her eyes sharpened on him with all seriousness. "Please don't cut me out of this investigation. Don't tell Stewart or Trevor or any of them."

He took a deep breath and turned at the next right. Off in the distance, Wheeler Peak glistened against the sun's rays and reached to the sky. The Sangre de Cristo mountain range shot up out of the flat plains surrounding it, expressing dominance over this portion of the state. As Jett toyed with the idea of making a way for Nic to be part of this next call, he wondered how she had earned her dominance in this case. Why was Don allowing her to take control when she had no jurisdiction? The department wasn't his concern, though.

"I'm the head of Search and Rescue. My sole job is to get people to safety. Willingly allowing you to go in when there is a prominent chance that you will buckle under pressure goes against all I strive to do."

"It's on me."

"Until someone else gets hurt because of you," he stated firmly.

She turned back to stare out the window again. He noticed her fists clenched in her lap, and when she spoke, her hardness was back. "I know you think I'm a horrible person, but my reasons to stay on this case outweigh the risks. What happened back there was more about me getting sloppy. After seeing the… the marriage license, I had a lapse in judgment and let down my guard."

Jett kept his eyes straight ahead, but sensed the paper in the breast pocket of his jacket. It felt scalding next to his chest, right over his heart. He turned his thoughts to the task at hand.

Find the suspect.

The drive-by shooter's car belonged to an address two streets away. Jett had a decision to make. "I probably will regret this." He took the next turn and stopped at the second house on the right. Trevor's cruiser was already here and parked across the street. He put the truck in Park and sighed deeply.

Nic turned his way, an expectant look on her face as she waited for his answer. If he said no, he doubted she would listen anyway.

"This will be the last chance. If you freeze up one more time, I'm going to the sheriff. I'm pretty sure he'll go to your supervisor."

As expected, her face paled instantly. He had his answer. Her involvement went beyond helping her father. Nicole Harrington had her own reputation to protect.

She gave a single nod and opened the passenger door. Before stepping outside, she surveyed the area behind her and then the house.

"I think it's safe to go. I'll meet you at the front of the car and we will approach the house together. Do not leave my side under any circumstances."

"It seems like a pretty quiet neighborhood," she said when he met her at the hood. Trevor stepped out of his car and joined them.

He said to Jett, "Are you sure you caught

that license plate right? This place is for retired people," he informed them as they approached the house. "Not much goes on
around here except maybe a game of pinochle
on the weekends."

"So this is not your typical neighborhood
that houses murderers?" Jett said.

Nic unclipped her holster at her back.
"Murderers come in all types. Never under-
estimate anyone."

Already he could see her stature change
into a powerful agent. She'd stayed by his
side but each step she walked was purposeful
and strong. When they came to the steps, he
allowed her to go up first. Trevor stood beside him on the sidewalk. She rang the door-
bell as Jett scanned the streets to their right
and left. But no sound came from inside the
house. She rang the bell again and tapped on
the metal door.

"Hang on," the voice of an old woman responded. "I'm not as young as I used to be.
Cut me some slack."

The door opened to reveal a woman in her
early eighties, less than five feet tall. She
wore her white hair in a big bun on top of
her head. She carried no glasses, but she did
squint up at them. "Yes?"

Being the uniformed officer, Trevor spoke

first. "I'm Deputy Mirabel, and this is Special Agent Harrington and Mr. Butler from Search and Rescue."

Jett peered behind the woman for evidence of another person in hiding.

"We are looking for Edward Hansen. He's the owner of a blue Nissan Altima," Nic said.

The woman's face fell, the loose skin trembling at the corners of her mouth. "My husband is no longer with me. He passed away last month."

"I'm sorry to hear that, ma'am—uh, Mrs. Hansen?" Jett caught Nic looking back at him, but he waited for the old woman to answer.

"Yes, Barb Hansen is my name. What is this all about? Why does Eddie's car concern you?"

Nic asked, "Is your husband's car here?"

Barb shook her head as tears sprang to her eyes. "I haven't seen it in a month."

"It was stolen?" Jett surmised.

Barb sighed and frowned. "No, not exactly. My son has it. He comes by every now and then, and the last time was right after Eddie's death. He skipped the funeral but stopped in after, saying he needed the car for a little while. That little while has now turned into month. I don't mind him taking the car. I'm not driving much anymore. It's that our relationship is strained, and I fear without Eddie here, I will never see Saul again."

"Saul?" Jett asked. "Saul Hansen is your son's name?" He tried to place the name but didn't find it familiar. "And you haven't seen him in a month? Have you spoken to him?"

Barb stepped back and put her hand on the door. "If he's done something, I'm sorry, but I can't help you. I can't help him, either. I suppose I never could."

Nic reached out her hand and placed it on Barb's forearm. Her bright yellow cardigan had pilled with age. "I'm sorry to hear you have had a falling out with your son. I know family relationships are not always perfect."

Barb covered Nic's hand with her own. "Thank you, my dear. I tried for years to make Saul part of our family. We fostered him when he was a teenager. That was thirty years ago now. Eddie and I couldn't have children, but had so much love to give. But just because we have that love doesn't mean we get it right. I fear our mistakes left Saul lacking and missing out, but his previous foster homes failed him, also."

"And you have no idea where he is now?" Nic asked.

"I'm not sure where he's living, but I do

know that he works part-time as an adjunct professor over at the community college. He's teaching a business class, I believe."

"You have a photo of your son?"

Barb took another step back. "I don't, and that's all I can tell you today. I'm sorry, but I have to go now." With that, Barb stepped back again and closed the door. The click of the lock turned over.

"We could get a warrant," Jett said as they walked back to Trevor's cruiser.

Trevor nodded. "The car is registered to her deceased husband. I'm sure I could have a judge's signature for one by the end today."

Nic crossed her arms. "We'll probably need it, but let's wait to see what kind of information I can get at the school first. The more we can put on a warrant, the better chance we'll have of making the charge stick."

"All right, boss," Trevor said. "Do you mind going to the school without me? I'll get started on looking for the car."

"Sounds good," Nic said, and the three parted ways.

Jett stayed close to Nic until he came around to his driver's side and climbed in. Tank gave a low woof in the back seat once the doors closed and they'd buckled in. As they drove down the street in silence, Jett thought again about how Sheriff Stewart had allotted Nic authority the other night in the lodge. Apparently, he wasn't the only one to allow her to take charge. Trevor now did the same. "May I ask you a question?"

Nic glanced his way and nodded. "Shoot."

"Was small-town police work always your goal—I mean, before the accident?"

She shrugged. "We were a team. That was the goal, no matter where we ended up."

Jett hadn't expected that answer. "Working with anyone is foreign to me. I work alone."

"That wasn't always the case," she stated. "There was a time you would have laid down your life for your partner."

"Because you were my partner?"

Nic turned away to look out the window again.

After a moment, she answered, "No. Because that was the kind of person you were."

NINE

The local community college on Friday afternoon appeared abandoned. Nic walked through the empty halls and peered into vacant classrooms. Jett stayed close by as he, too, surveyed the building for signs of life.

"With no one at the front desk and no security, I have to question the running of the school," he said.

"There aren't too many college classes held on Friday afternoons this late. We may have to wait until Monday to speak with anyone in the office." Nic headed for a long hallway off the main one. Ahead, she saw a sign for the office of the dean. As they drew closer, she noticed a light. "Here we go."

They stepped inside. There was no one at the receptionist's desk, so Nic walked around it. "Hello?" She knocked on the office door that had a nameplate with the name Mark Donovan on it.

"Yes?" a male voice said from within. "How can I help you?" The sound of a chair squeaked just before the office door swung open.

The dean of the college appeared a bit disheveled with his tie loosened and top two shirt buttons not secured. But it was Friday afternoon, and all had gone home.

"I'm sorry to bother you. Are you Mark Donovan?"

"Yes, I am. I'm the dean of students." He eyed them both. "Are you looking to register for classes?"

"No, I'm Special Agent Harrington, FBI, and this is Jett Butler. We have some questions about a certain adjunct professor at the school."

"The FBI?" The dean stood back to let them in. There were two chairs in front of the desk, but Mark didn't invite them to sit. He kept them at the opened doorway in his office.

"I'm not here on official FBI business. I'm here to help the local sheriff's department with a crime committed on the mountain."

"You mean the helicopter crash? It was a crime?"

"The sheriff's office is considering all avenues," Jett interjected. "We're here to ask about Saul Hansen. We have some questions for him but are unsure of how to find him."

"Saul? Saul wouldn't be involved in that helicopter crash. He's one of our best accounting teachers. The students love him. They line up to be his assistant each semester."

Nic glanced at Jett then back at the dean. "Perhaps one of them could help us find him?"

"That would be highly unethical of me to provide names of students. I really can't give out information about where our teachers live, either. Unless you have some sort of warrant?"

Nic glanced at the desktop covered in papers and fast-food wrappers. Apparently, Dean Donovan wanted to play hardball. She grabbed his business card sitting in a container on the desk and scrawled out the Sheriff Department's number on the back. Handing it over to him, she said, "No need for a warrant at this time. He just might be a person of interest. We have a few questions we're hoping he can clear up. If you can pass along the sheriff's number, I would appreciate it."

Donovan took the card and looked at it. He stuffed it into the breast pocket of his wrinkled dress shirt, fumbling twice before the card made it inside. "Of course. Of course. I will do everything I legally can to help you."

Jett replied, "We appreciate it. The safety of our town depends on us figuring out the facts of this case."

The dean led them back out of his office. "Then I'll get to contacting him right away."

Nic recognized the man's swift adios, and Jett motioned for her to precede him. The dean stood back to let them pass but followed them out into the hall.

Something felt off, but there was not much else they could do. As they neared the exit to the building, Nic noticed the wall by the main door. She hadn't seen it when she'd entered earlier because it had been behind her. On the billboard there was a picture of each professor who taught at the school. A quick scan for the business department and she found herself staring at the face of the killer.

Air whooshed from her lungs, and her mouth went dry. The name below the picture: Saul Hansen.

Nic nudged Jett, hoping he could see the direction of her attention. To give him time to pick up on her cue and locate the picture, Nic turned around to face the dean.

"One more question, if you don't mind, Mr. Donovan." She didn't let him respond and quickly continued. "You mentioned Mr. Hansen hired teacher's aides each semester. What kind of work do these aides typically do?"

Nic moved to the side so Donovan would have to turn to follow her. He looked like he was worried she would return to his office.

"The aides help with correcting papers and such. They can also teach the classes if they are equipped, but usually they assist the professors with time-consuming tasks to help the class run smoothly."

Nic eyed Jett studying the wall. She silently prayed that he would locate the correct picture in the sea of teachers. "Thank you. If I have any other questions, I will be in touch. We will head out, unless you have something to ask, Mr. Butler?" Nic asked and leaned her head toward the wall, hoping he would understand her subtlety. "Do you have all you need?"

"Yes," Jett stated firmly. "I have everything I need." He turned away from the wall. "Thank you, Dean Donovan, for your time."

"I sure hope you clear up whatever happened up there on the mountain. We all thought it was a tragic accident. I still hope that's all it was."

"We hope so, too." Jett ushered Nic out by her elbow. They didn't say a word until they were finally back in the car, when Nic said, "Saul Hansen is the killer."

"You're positive?" She nodded. "He needs to be picked up immediately. He's armed and dangerous."

Jett got on the radio and contacted the sheriff.

"You're sure about this, Nic?" Sheriff Stewart asked.

"Positive."

"If that's the case, I'm going to release the teams from the resort. I'll order an all-points bulletin, and we'll pick him up in town then. Good work."

They gave him the car model, a name and an ID. But they had no idea where Saul was living.

"Maybe one of his aides knows how to find him," Nic said after Jett disconnected the radio call.

Jett took the road to the mountain. "That would only help if Donovan was talking."

"Or we had a warrant. With my positive ID, we must have enough probable cause."

Jett nodded but drove in the direction of Wild Mountain.

"Why are we going to the resort? If we can get into his office at the school, I'm sure we will have the lead we need to find him."

"Because it's the safest place for you. I have Saul's ID now."

Air rushed from her lips. Sickening anger flipped her stomach. "Meaning you don't need me anymore."

His jaw ticked. "If that's how you want to see it, so be it. Believe it or not, it's about your safety. In case you haven't realized it yet, Saul Hansen wants you dead. He *needs* you dead. I won't parade you around like a target."

Nic huffed. "You don't have the final say in that. I'm not sure if anyone ever told you, but when we worked together, I outranked you. I still do." She was already making plans to speak to the sheriff. Jett didn't know how Sheriff Stewart owed her. Jett was in for a big surprise.

Jett knew that Nic had taken his direction personally. He reminded himself that that was why he worked alone. He lacked finesse in explaining his reasons. Struggling with framing his words eloquently was why he'd pushed his family away from him, as well. He wondered if he'd been like this before the accident. He had to think it was a new personality trait. Otherwise, his family would've left him long before the accident. Who wants to be around an ill-tempered bear?

Tank jumped to the frontseat and barked as they watched Nic enter the lodge. She practically stomped all the way from the car. The woman was on a mission to put him in his place. He would take whatever she dished out if it meant he wouldn't have to watch her go down the way she had at his house.

He stepped from his truck as his chest constricted at the memory from just hours ago. Seeing her sprawled on the ground, frozen, splintered something in his mind. He couldn't put his finger on it, and it made no sense. He had no recollection of this woman, and yet, seeing her being shot at caused his anxiety to skyrocket. He'd yet to take a deep breath. He doubted he would again until this guy was caught.

Jett pulled open the heavy wooden door to the lodge and let Tank go in. Christmas lights strung from the rafters and around the lobby brought a peaceful atmosphere to a desolate place.

"I need to open, or I'm going to go under," Les was saying to his daughter at the staircase. "You haven't been here. You don't know how hard we have been hit. I can't keep up with the other resorts in their newfangled enclosed chairlifts. I'm old school. All I know is how things used to be done. If my doors don't open now, they will never be opened again."

"I'm sorry, Pop, you should have told me you needed help here." Nic reached for her father's arm.

Les allowed Nic to touch him, but he leaned away from her and toward Dahlia on his right.

Dahlia said, "Come on, you two. Why don't we sit by the fire and have some hot cocoa?"

Les huffed. "Who's going to pay for that? The two of you don't get this. There's no money left."

"Pop, I was looking for your ledger. I want to help if I can. Let me see where we might be able to cut back. I'm here for a few more weeks. We'll get you through the season."

"You're two seasons too late. I shouldn't have even opened this year. Now I'm so far under. I need to open to recoup some of my losses." Les looked at Jett as he and Tank approached the three of them. "Tell Sheriff Stewart to let me open."

Jett cleared his throat. "I'm sorry to hear you've been struggling. We have a killer on the loose. He is armed and dangerous. He came after your daughter again today. It's best if there is no one on this mountain. A crowd of people would make protecting her near impossible."

"Oh, honey, what happened?" Dahlia stepped closer to Nic. "Are you hurt?" Her gaze did a once-over before searching Nic's face for an answer.

"I'm fine, Dahlia. The guy has horrible aim."

If she thought that was funny, nobody laughed.

Jett held his annoyed opinion in check. He glanced at Les, but the man was looking at his watch. If he was concerned about his daughter, he wasn't letting on. The man was preoccupied. His wispy, thinning hair was disheveled and in need of a comb.

"Les—" Dahlia turned to him "—why don't we start over? We're all adults here. Come, sit by the fire and discuss this." Dahlia urged them all to find seats by the flickering flames at the center of the room.

"There's nothing to discuss," Les said, though he did take the seat Dahlia had led him to. "I'm opening tomorrow and that's the end of it."

The way the old man sat, in a rigid pose and facing away from his daughter, Jett wondered about the distance between them. Had their relationship always been this tense? A glance at Nic's acceptance of it made him think this was normal. Jett thought about Nic's words at Saul Hansen's mother's house.

She'd consoled the woman with understanding about familial tensions. If this tension was somewhat new between Nic and her father, then perhaps Les was involved in something that was causing him to withdraw from the relationship.

"Pop, I meant what I said. Let me see your bookkeeping." Nic leaned forward toward her father. Her pleading didn't move him.

Jett realized what she was aiming for. She hadn't located that ledger. They had searched the office, and it was nowhere to be found.

"I have Dahlia now to help me. And I've hired an accountant," Les said. "We don't need someone else mucking around with our numbers."

"I'm glad you have Dahlia," Nic said. With no smile on her face, Jett wondered how glad she really was. "But I'm not just anyone. I'm your daughter. Please don't push me away."

"Dahlia and I are getting married," Les announced abruptly.

"Oh, Les," Dahlia said quietly. "Now is not the time to announce this. There's so much going on, and Nicole needs our support and protection." She looked at Nic. "This isn't how I wanted to share this news with you." Dahlia sighed. "But I suppose with everything going on here, there might not be a better time."

Nic began to speak but stopped. A shocked expression rippled across her face. Her gaze locked on her father. "I... I see." She stood. The palms of her hands trembled against her thighs. "This is a big surprise." She swallowed hard. Her eyes glistened. "I'm happy for you both. Really."

Dahlia jumped up, wringing her hands. "This wasn't how I wanted this to be. But please, know that I love your father very much. We do make each other very happy. I want to get to know you more. I'm not here to cut you out of your father's life in any way."

Nic nodded. She looked to her father and lifted her chin. "Congratulations, Pop."

Les frowned. "I should've told you when you first arrived. There's no reason to keep secrets. Of course you can help with the bookkeeping. The ledger's in the office."

Nic glanced at Jett. "Is it in a special place? I didn't notice it with the others."

Les's gaze hardened. "So you've already been snooping?"

"I was hardly snooping. I wanted to see if there were places to cut back. That's all."

Les stood and walked to the office. Jett expected him to open the door. Instead, he reached under the counter and withdrew a ring of keys. Before Jett realized what Les was about to do, he slipped a key into the door and locked it.

Les turned back to the room, but only looked at his daughter. "When I want your help, I'll ask for it." He then looked at Jett. "Tell Sheriff Stewart I open tomorrow."

Dahlia whined. "But, Les, what about your daughter's safety?"

He grunted. "She didn't deem it necessary to contact me the first time she got shot. Why should this time be any different?" With that, Les walked past them and up the stairs.

Tank lifted his head and, with everybody else, watched him go. His whimper spoke to them all.

Dahlia seemed conflicted but chose to go after Les, the click of her heels racing up the wooden steps, her long ponytail swinging side to side.

A door slammed somewhere off in the lodge and silence fell on the room. Once alone, Jett braved the question. "Did you really not notify him when you were in the hospital?"

Nic still faced the locked office door. She turned her head slightly his way, just enough for him to observe the look he hadn't seen on her face since the moment they'd met on the mountaintop.

Defeat.

This woman had had guns pointed at her and triggers pulled. She'd even taken one of those bullets. He'd seen her hang from a ledge to retrieve evidence. And, no matter what, she'd bravely faced danger head-on. It was now, in this moment, that he could see her father had the power to defeat her.

"I keep forgetting you don't remember what it was like for me to live here," she said quietly. "There were many times you were there for me when I felt his rejection." She swallowed hard. "Up until the moment I felt yours."

Jett bit back a retort and let out a sigh. He let her have her dig because he knew it had nothing to do with him and went much deeper. "I'm sorry to hear that, and I'm sorry if you feel I let you down in the process. I had no way of knowing."

She faced him directly. The tilt to her chin told him her courage was returning. "You pushed me away again today, by wanting me to hide out here. If you are truly sorry, then stop trying to stop me from being involved."

"This isn't the time for dealmaking," Jett said.

"I'm not making a deal. I'm asking for an

opportunity to mend fences in the only way I know how. I don't have the feminine instincts that my mother had. Or that Dahlia has. I was never able to be that replacement for my mom to my father."

"So this animosity began after your mom passed away?"

She nodded. "But it was never this tense and vindictive."

Jett glanced at staircase. "You didn't even notify him about your GSW. Perhaps he felt hurt that you left him out of it."

"I was unconscious. Then I spent months in rehab. There was no reason to alert him once I was out of the woods. When it was safe for me to travel, I called him and came back here."

Jett shrugged. "A phone call when it happened might have been nice. Just saying."

"Maybe." She chewed on her lower lip. "Honestly, I didn't think he would care." She let out quick breath and shrugged it off. "It's whatever. I can't change the past, but I can stop this guy in his tracks. That's what I aim to do while I am here."

Jett sighed. "Remember what I said earlier in the truck. If I see you freeze up in any way, I will post a guard at your door. Do you understand?"

"If I freeze up one more time, I will turn in my badge and gun." Her declaration stunned him.

Jett gave a single nod. "I'll go check on that warrant. Be ready to ride."

"Always," she mumbled. Her gaze drifted to the office door. "What if…"

Jett could see the workings of her mind play out on her face. She was beginning to doubt her father's innocence. "Don't go there. Not yet."

"The cop in me says I have to." She looked at Jett and shoved up out of her chair. "Be prepared to get a second warrant." She left him and headed to the stairs, her back straight, her head high. It took a strong individual to be willing to put the law above family.

Jett was beginning to learn just how strong Nic Harrington was. Something he would have known ten years ago if he had allowed her to stick around.

Or perhaps sending her away was what had strengthened her.

Or hardened her.

A feeling of guilt swept over him. Nic's father played a role in her tough edge. But then, so did he. Admiring her for her resolve didn't feel right. Not when it came about by causing her so much pain.

Tank whined, staring after Nic as she disappeared upstairs. His ears perked up, and he sent questioning eyes Jett's way.

Jett whistled, and the dog came trouncing over to him for a pat. His piercing eyes held questions as he tilted his head. "I'm worried about her, too," Jett said. "Something tells me she's about to do something foolish…again."

TEN

Jett had told her not to let her mind go there, but how could she not? Her father had made it quite clear that she was not welcome to view his books. She wasn't even welcome to enter his office now. He either really distrusted her or he was hiding something. Could he be involved in criminal activities? The thought had her pacing back and forth in her private room.

Growing up at the ski lodge had always been a unique situation. While her friends had homes and yards that were for them only, Nic had had to share her home and yard with visitors every day and night.

The Harrington family's private living quarters were sequestered at the back of the lodge, away from the hotel rooms. There was a small kitchen and living room, as well as their bedrooms. Since returning home, Nic had yet to see her father in any of the rooms. She'd assumed he'd chosen to stay in one of the rented suites, and as she walked through the living area toward his typical bedroom, the one he'd shared with her mother, she wondered how long ago he had moved out of their private quarters.

Nic reached for the knob to his bedroom door. She knew it was unlocked; when she'd first arrived home, she had opened it to find it empty. Once again, she stood in the open doorway, but this time she stepped inside.

Never before had she felt the need to snoop on her father. Searching through his room felt like a violation of trust. So much of the space reminded of her of her mother. Her feminine touch was everywhere. This was a room that did not belong in the rustic lodge. For the first time, Nic realized Claire Harrington's femininity permeated the walls of her husband's ruggedness. Les Harrington may be able to live outdoors for days on end, but when he entered this room, he would be reminded that there was another way to live. A more gentle way.

Nic traced her finger across the Victorian dresser. Dust from many months came away. She walked past the canopy bed and felt the smooth railing at the foot. Floral pillow shams held the memory of the lilac scent of her mother's perfume. Nic approached the nightstand. The lampshade with fringe tickled her wrist as she turned on the light. The darkened room quickly softened in its a warm glow.

She turned to face her mother's writing desk. The cover was closed tight, its antique chair with the red plush cushion tucked in close. Nic pulled it out and sat. She raised the lid of the desk and folded it back. For a few seconds, she just stared at a moment frozen in time. It didn't look like her father had touched anything in twenty years. Claire Harrington's personal effects remained still. Old letters filled the upper slats. Yellowed stationery, tucked into a box, waited for its owner to pen the next letter. A letter that would never come.

Nic pulled open the drawer in front of her. Her mother's diary was placed perfectly straight inside. She rubbed her fingertips across the leather cover. She had come in looking for a ledger that would reveal her father's doings. Instead, she'd found her mother's.

Nic opened the diary cover and inhaled at the sight of her mother's penmanship. Every letter was perfectly angled in a sweep of graceful style. Even in her writing, she'd exuded femininity. She was everything Nic

fought against being. A quick scan of the first
entry depicted her mother's peaceful exis-
tence on the mountain and her daily activities. If she was unhappy, it was not portrayed
in her writing. Her love for her husband had
always been obvious, even if they had been
so drastically different.

Nic flipped through a few pages, pausing
at one when she saw her name.

*Nicole is so much stronger than I've
ever been. She takes after her father in
so many ways. But I worry that in her
strength, she won't realize she needs
God. Without Him, she will always
struggle to be the best just so she will
be accepted.*

Nic quickly slammed the diary shut, closed
the drawer swiftly and stood. Her heart rate
picked up to a rapid pace.

"That's what I get for snooping," she said
aloud as she tucked the chair into place. Some
things were better left unknown. Reading her
mother's thoughts about her would only lead
to conjecture and too many unanswered questions. Staying focused on finding the ledger
was all that mattered right now.

Scanning the rest of the room, Nic walked

to the dresser and opened each drawer one by one. Nothing of her father's remained, which confirmed for her that he had been out of this room for a while. Moving to the closet, she opened the door and found more of the same. There was no sense looking for the ledger in here. He either had it with him, or it was still in the office somewhere. The fact that he'd locked the door made her think it was in there, that she had just missed it somehow.

With one last look around, Nic pulled the bedroom door closed and walked out of the private quarters.

She made her way through the dark halls that typically had people coming and going but were now eerily desolate. She noticed that the sconces, usually aglow both day and night had been all dimmed low. Perhaps her father had done that to save on electricity. His lack of funds would explain his soured demeanor toward her, she thought as she made her way to the lobby. Maybe she had stayed away too long.

Nic frowned. Of course she had stayed away too long. She thought of her mother's written words. Had she neglected her father in an attempt to belong, to be accepted in her career? Had she attempted to create a family outside of the one she'd already had?

She opened the door to the lodge lobby and froze. The room was cloaked in darkness. All the Christmas lights had been turned off, and the fire had gone out. She slowly made her way to the stairs. She felt for the banister and let it guide her way down, step by step. When she reached the landing, she squinted to look through the darkness.

"Jett? Are you here?" Perhaps he was sleeping on one of the sofas. She took a few steps in and trained her ear to listen for any sounds. As far as she could tell, she was completely alone. She made her way over to the check-in counter, feeling the wall beside it for the light switches. As soon as her fingertips reached the panel, she flipped them up.

Nothing happened.

A few more flips, but everything stayed the same.

A busted fuse? Maybe? She walked in front of the counter, closer to the couches against the wall. "Jett?" she called out again, louder. *Where is he?*

Suddenly an idea came to mind. Had the police gotten the warrant and Jett left without her? Irritation skyrocketed within her. She marched over to the main doors and found them locked.

He had left.

But more, he had left her behind.

Nic took a moment to think of her next steps. Jett had warned her that he worked alone. She shouldn't be surprised that he would take off without her.

She vowed to remember this.

She turned to head back to her quarters, but before she could take a step, something behind her alerted her to someone's presence. She froze and listened intently. It had sounded like a creak in a floorboard. Without a noise, she pivoted to face where the sound had come from. The check-in desk stood in the darkness before her. Her first steps were muffled as she moved toward it. Circling around the desk, the wood floor cracked beneath her weight. She lifted her foot and stepped over the revealing board onto a quieter one. The office door was about five steps away. She took each one carefully.

Nic thought about checking the doorknob to see if it was still locked. She reasoned that that would give her presence away, so she leaned her ear close to the door.

A scraping sound from inside claimed her attention. It wasn't the sound of chairs being moved. No, it was more like a window scraping. As if someone was closing a window, or more likely, opening it. Time was critical if she wanted to catch whoever was inside the office. She had only seconds to make a decision. Bypassing the doorknob, she took two steps back and lifted her leg high. With all her strength, she kicked out, splintering the wooden door in one move. At the same time, her motion thrust her forward and she used her shoulder to drive through any remaining pieces of wood. Moonlight cast shadows in the room, and at the window, a person's leg was left inside as they climbed on the counter to get out.

"Freeze! FBI!" Nic raced over and grabbed hold of the leg before the intruder disappeared.

With only the moonbeams streaming in through the two windows, she had no way of knowing who the person was. Her single focus was to get them back inside and find out.

With all her might, she pulled the intruder back through the window and threw them to the floor. Even though it was dark, she knew it was a man.

"Give yourself up, Hansen," she ordered into the dark room. "We already have a warrant. It's over."

In a split second, the intruder rammed into her midsection, sending her against the counter along the wall with the windows. The man's forearm shoved her backward and pressed against her neck. She heard herself gurgling and gasping for air. She lifted her knee and jammed it up and into his abdomen. It was enough to gain a reprieve from his arm and twist free of his grasp. Nic kicked out, weakening his thigh enough to bring him to his knees. She grabbed his arm to bring it around his back to apprehend him only to feel instant pain across the side of her head. He'd hit her with something hard. It felt like a brick.

All sense of reason flew from her mind. Whatever he'd used landed to her right with a thud on the floor. It took her a moment to realize she was facedown by the desk chair and that the sound might have been her.

"Nic!" Jett's voice came from the lobby.

She opened her mouth, but all she could do was make a croaking sound. She heard shuffling around her and the intruder murmuring to himself. Then footsteps closed in as Jett neared the office, and the man jumped up onto the counter to make his escape again.

Nic pushed up onto her elbows and tried to bend her knees to rise. Her head swirled and pain forced her to drop back down. "Window," she rasped.

A hand felt around her until the fingers touched her shoulder. "Are you all right?" Jett asked.

"Yes," she said. "Go. Find him."

"I don't want to leave you," Jett mumbled in his struggle to stay or go.

"I'm okay," she assured him. "Before he disappears, get out there!"

"Tank, stay!"

With that, Jett stood and jumped up onto the counter and followed the man out the window. She could hear the swooshing of fresh fallen snow as he plowed through it in pursuit.

Tank sat beside Nic as she sat upright and took a moment to clear her head. She needed light to maneuver around the office. Remembering seeing a flashlight in the drawer, she crawled over to it and felt her way to opening it. The flashlight was right where she remembered, and she flicked it on. Turning back, she circled the beam across the floor until she found what she had been hit with.

She gained her footing and walked slowly over to a large book. As she picked it up, she knew exactly what it was.

The missing ledger.

It would appear she hadn't been the only one looking for it.

* * *

Jett barreled through the deep snow, following the tracks the intruder had left behind. The frigid night air burned his throat with shallow and quick breaths. He expected the tracks to lead toward the parking lot, but instead they ascended the mountain. He pushed harder to reach the guy before he lost him. As he approached the chairlift house, he heard the motor of a snowmobile start up. Once on the slope, the snow wasn't as deep. It had been compressed and groomed for ideal skiing conditions tomorrow, but that also meant the snowmobile's tracks weren't as obvious, especially in the dark.

Following the sound of the cranking engine, Jett ran through a cluster of trees. Branches swiped at his face, but he kept moving forward. He burst through the last of the trees just in time to see the man put the snowmobile into gear and start moving.

Jett took one giant leap and managed to grab hold of the guy's coat. With all his strength, he held on as the snowmobile picked up speed. Jett's fingers burned in the cold night air. He didn't know how long he could hold on, given his feet were dragging behind him and being tossed around. His chest bounced against the rear of the machine, knocking the wind out of him with each bump along the route.

As the snowmobile moved upward and the angle made climbing harder, Jett used all his strength to secure one of his feet on the back while he held onto the guy's coat. Once there, he pushed up on that leg to gain a foothold with the other. Just as he tried to sit on the back, the guy made a sharp right that sent Jett flying through the air. For a split second, he watched the snowmobile's taillights get farther away right before he landed on his back in a hard mound of snow.

Jett grunted on impact, then growled and threw snow in the direction of the retreating snowmobile. Higher and higher it went, to an unknown location. If that was Saul Hansen, then perhaps he wasn't staying in town at all but rather on the mountain. If he was hiding out at Wild Mountain somewhere, then opening up to skiers come sunup wouldn't be an option.

Now to get Les to understand that letting skiers on the slopes could be deadly.

Jett stood and dusted off the layer of snow from his jeans. With one last look up to where the snowmobile disappeared, he turned and headed back to the lodge. He thought about getting a team up there, but the guy would be long gone before he could round people up. Perhaps a better strategy would be to barricade the guy in place until they could find him.

For now, Jett needed to make sure Nic was okay. He picked up his pace and didn't slow until he was back inside the lodge and standing beside her.

"Is that what I think it is?" he asked, looking at a large book open in her lap.

She sat on the couch beside the circle hearth where a fire now slightly brightened the dark room and danced flickering shadows on the walls and across Nic's face. She held a flashlight above a page of numbers. "It sure is." She didn't sound too excited. She looked up at him, and in the firelight, he could see tears glistening in her eyes.

"Do I need a warrant, or will you allow me to see?" he asked before attempting a look. The spot beside her on the couch would remain vacant until she invited him. As seconds ticked by, he wondered if she would.

"When you woke up in the hospital and didn't recognize anyone, did you want to close your eyes and pretend it was all a dream?"

He didn't answer her question, wondering where she was going with this train of thought. Jett shrugged and searched for the answer she might be looking for. "I suppose there were times I wished I knew who this Jethro Butler was that they were looking for. If that's what you mean."

"Because you wanted to be him, or to just pretend so you could keep the peace?"

Jett held back the sickening laugh building up inside of him. "Do you really need to relive those days to realize I would never want to be part of a façade? I chose the truth. I chose the truth, even knowing the consequences. I didn't know anyone, and I wasn't going to pretend to know them—or myself. What does all this have to do with that ledger?" He looked to the book in her lap.

She pressed her lips tight. "I feel like I've just woken up, and I don't recognize my father. I can either pretend he is the man I grew up with, or I can accept he has changed into someone I don't know."

"And you want to know what happens if you choose the truth?" Jett took the seat beside her. He kept a few feet of distance between them, not wanting to crowd her in this moment of disappointment. His heart longed to bring comfort to her, but he wasn't sure where that had come from and rejected the idea instantly. That was not his role, and he wouldn't pretend otherwise.

Nic stared into the fire. Her eyes drifted closed on a sigh. "I was on the receiving end when you chose the truth. I know what happens. I know all about the consequences that came out of your choice." She opened her eyes and looked at him. Her lips trembled as a tear slipped down her cheek. "For ten years, I lived with anger over your choice. But right now, I want to thank you for having the courage to make it. You made the right choice." She gulped and said, "And now, I have to as well." She passed the ledger over to his lap.

Her decision weighed heavy on him, knowing the traitorous feeling she was having. He knew it well and didn't wish it on anyone, especially her.

Jett wondered why he thought of her differently, but again, rejected any validation of his thoughts. She was just another cop. That was all. But even as he thought it, he hesitated in opening the book. "Perhaps I should look at this in private."

"I've already seen everything." Her frown told him it wasn't good.

He put his hand out for the flashlight. "You mind?" He had the ledger open before she placed the light in his hand.

"It begins a year ago. Right where the other one left off." She pointed to one entry about the helicopter. "About six months ago, he started renting things. He's been renting it to…" Her voice cracked. After she cleared her throat, she said, "Well, you can see who he is renting it to. Among other things."

Jett scanned across the page to the recipient. The name Saul Hansen stopped him cold. "This doesn't mean anything," he assured her. "Anyone could rent the helicopter. Your father wouldn't be able to know what everyone was doing with it."

"Keep reading," she said. "There are other things."

Jett looked at the ledger and moved his finger to the next entry. "'Cabin rental,'" he read. "What cabin? There are rooms to rent in the lodge, but I didn't know there were cabins, as well."

"There's not. There's only one." Her eyes widened then grew sad. "Ours. The one you built for us."

Jett looked in the direction of the house he had built and realized it was on the same path the snowmobile had raced off to. Now he knew where the guy had been heading, where he had been staying for at least the last month.

Jett looked at the date of the rental. The first entry was six months ago. But as he flipped the pages, he could see every month had another entry. He slid his finger across the page to see the price. And choked. He looked at the other entries and saw that they were the same.

"Your father rents the cabin for fifty thousand a month?" The idea seemed preposterous.

No, not preposterous, but criminal.

"He's laundering money, isn't he?" she asked. But what answer could he give her that she didn't already know? There would be no assuring her of anything else.

"Don't jump to any conclusions."

"There are also payments to people that I don't know." She pointed to a name in the middle of the page. A woman named Francesca Sylvan. "Why is she getting money separate from the other employees who get paid from payroll?" Nic turned the page and pointed to another name. "And what about this Tina Brunson? Who are these women?"

Jett had no answer and, until he apprehended Saul Hansen, he wouldn't. "I need to get to the cabin. Now." He stood. "I can only assume that was Saul fighting you for this ledger. I tried to tackle him on the snowmobile, but he headed up the mountain. Now I know where he was going. The sheriff needs to get his teams back out here immediately. But I'm not waiting for them."

Nic looked up at him and nodded. "I'm going with you."

"No, you're not. You are to stay here, and don't mention anything to your father. I know you don't want to pretend, but I'm going to ask you to until I get back."

Jett walked over to the desk to call in reinforcements. Once he relayed the orders to the dispatcher, he turned back and growled.

Nic was busying herself putting the fire out. She lifted a bucket of water that was kept by the hearth.

He didn't have to ask why. "If anyone gets hurt because you freeze up, I will—"

She cut him off with an assurance she had no business offering. "No one will get hurt."

"That goes for you, too," Jett said, making sure she understood his warning included her. "Your well-being is my concern. It's always been my concern. It may not have felt that way when I asked you to leave that day in the hospital, but lying to you wasn't the answer, either."

Her eyes locked onto his. The dying embers cast shadows on her stunned face, caused by his admitting that pushing her away ten years ago hadn't been a personal rejection of her, but rather the best way to not hurt her in the long run.

Nic poured out the last of the water and extinguished the fire. Darkness once again cloaked the room and shrouded their faces from each other.

"I want to believe that, but my memory of that day says otherwise. You hurt me." She sounded so small. Gone was the deep strength her voice typically exuded. But even as quiet as she spoke, her last words echoed in his head long after she left the room.

ELEVEN

Nic sat shotgun in Jett's truck with Tank in the back again. The road to their cabin twisted up the mountain, and in the middle of winter, it was barely one lane. They'd hitched up the snowmobile trailer in case they couldn't get through with the truck. She hoped they wouldn't have to use them and that they would arrive at the alpine lake house quickly with no hindrances.

Jett barely made it to the halfway point before they realized their access was blocked, but not by snow. A gigantic tree had fallen across the road, leaving no way to get around it. He pulled the truck up close and put it into Park.

"End of the line," he said. "I wonder if Les knows there is a tree blocking the road. There is no way the team will be able to get up here tonight."

Nic thought of her father's secretive behavior. "There's a lot he's not being upfront about. Earlier, I figured out he hasn't been sleeping in the private quarters for months at least."

"Where is he sleeping?" Jett opened the driver's-side door and climbed out.

Nic joined him and met him at the back of the trailer. "I have no idea. I can only assume it's one of the rented rooms."

Jett opened the doors to reveal the two snowmobiles. "Don't assume anything. The lodge is a big place. No need to be concerned right now."

"I'll let it go, for now." She looked up into the dark road ahead of them. On the other side of the fallen tree, they still had a few miles to go before they reached the cabin. "But with each thing I am learning, it feels like my father is keeping me out in the cold." She waved at the tree trunk lit up by the truck's headlights. The dark night beyond promised a frigid excursion. "And now, literally."

"You can return to the lodge. In fact, that would be the best—"

"Not a chance." Nic moved to suit up for the ride. The two of them put on their snow pants and protective gear.

As Jett removed the snow machines from the trailer, headlights beamed from behind them. Three trucks pulled up, and Sheriff Stewart stepped out of one of them. With the engines still on and the headlights ablaze, the area could be better viewed.

"I don't believe in coincidences," Sheriff Stewart said. "This tree trunk is too convenient."

"Nic and I are going to head up on the snowmobiles. How quick can you get a team up there?" Jett asked. "I'd like to know backup will be quickly behind us."

"Give us thirty minutes."

"Not a moment longer. This guy is most likely expecting us. He knows we have the ledger, and his name is written all over it."

Sheriff Stewart looked at Nic. "I'm sorry to see you have to go through this. Jett informed me about the ledger's contents. I'm in shock, as well. Les was a good man."

Nic climbed onto the snowmobile. After she put the helmet over her head, she lifted the visor. "He still is."

Sheriff replied, "I hope so. I hope there is a valid reason why he's working with this man and collecting large amounts of money from him. You have to admit, this doesn't look good."

Nic glanced at Jett as he and Tank climbed on their snowmobile beside her. "If there's anything I've learned tonight, it's that looks can be deceiving."

Sheriff said, "Looks, for sure, but not money. Money tells all. I've allowed you, Nic, to be part of this investigation, but you really don't have jurisdiction. With your father becoming suspicious, your time assisting us may be coming to an end." The sheriff turned and climbed back into his truck. It was obvious the man wouldn't be cutting Les some slack, and her time was running out.

All the more reason to get to the root perpetrator of the crime. Whatever Saul Hansen was into, he was using the cabin to do it. Nic was eager to get up there to find out what it was. The faster she did, the quicker she could help her father right this wrong. She held out hope that he had been conned in some way.

A flash from something he had said earlier surfaced in her mind. He had said something about having to do things he'd never thought he would. Did he mean criminally? She wasn't ready to think about it yet.

"Let's ride," she said to Jett and lowered her visor. "Time is short, and I'm not waiting." She'd spoken louder to be heard.

Tank poked his nose out from the hole in his travel case on the back seat and barked once.

"Do you have your gun handy?" Jett asked.

Nic motioned to where her sidearm was holstered and nodded. "I have it at the ready in case we run into a problem on the way up."

"Keep your head low and stay in front of me," he ordered.

"You're letting me lead the way?" Had she heard him correctly?

"No. I'm protecting your back. Now go." He lowered his visor, and she couldn't see his face to know if his words meant something more than being a good partner. He'd stunned her for a moment, but when she hit the throttle and took off to skirt the fallen tree, knowing he had her back gave her more confidence than she'd ever felt on the job. And Nic never thought she lacked any.

As the snowmobile screamed over the rough terrain and made tracks up the mountain, she wondered what else she would learn the truth about tonight.

As the pilot for Search and Rescue, Jett had flown over the cabin and lake many times, but he hadn't been inside for ten years. Not since his family had tried to make him remember by bringing him here. They'd told him how he'd spent every free moment there, building it and making it a home. No matter what they'd told him, he'd had no recollection or connection with the place. And yet a sense of irritation now stirred within him at the thought of the cabin being used for illegal activities.

In front of him, Nic led the way up the road. After the fallen tree, they hadn't run into any other holdups and were making record time. The cabin wasn't much farther. It should appear around the next bend at any second. Yet, something about this all felt too easy. Too convenient.

Too much like a setup.

Before Jett could alert Nic to slow down, the cabin appeared in the distance and she drove her snowmobile faster toward it.

Lights shone from the windows, still so small from far away. Smoke billowed from the chimney, portraying a quaint coziness that belied the danger inside. Jett flashed his headlight a few times, and Nic slowed to a stop and shut down her machine. He came up beside her and killed his engine, but left his headlight on.

In the still quiet, they lifted their visors. "This is as far as we go," he said and dismounted. She followed him. "I hope we haven't already given ourselves away."

"I'm pretty sure he was expecting us anyway. Do we wait for everyone else?"

"That would be wise," Jett said, surveying the land ahead. "We'll have to go on foot from here."

"We can't just walk up to the front door." Nic turned to peer into the dark woods. "The lake is to the left, but we may be able to come around the right if we cut through the trees. If we approach via the rear of the house, we could surprise him from behind. Or better yet, we could separate and go in from front and back doors. He won't be able to hold us both off."

Jett didn't like the idea of Nic advancing on her own. "We go in together or we don't go in at all. In fact, it might be best if we wait for backup. I am not a deputy anymore."

"Once a cop, always a cop. Tell me what you really want to do. The truth." She folded her arms in front of her. The way she held her body spoke of authority.

"The truth? The truth is I work alone. I'm no one's backup, and the only backup I have is my dog."

"Then why change your procedure? Do it. Don't worry about me. I'll get myself in there in the best way I know how. As long as you feel like you have to protect me, then you can't be at your best." She reached into her coat pocket and took out a folded piece of paper. She stood in front of the headlight and unfolded the paper. Looking into the darkness, she said, "The land drops down to some swampy water, but it should be frozen over enough to allow me to get up behind the house."

"Is that one of my brother's maps that you took from my box??" Jett stepped closer to her until he could see the lines drawn on the paper. She had torn it from the notebook with the others.

"And yours," she said. "You both drew these, and you were meticulous around this area. This was the land that we both chose..." She had left off the information that he'd been particularly meticulous about mapping this area because they were going to make it their home. Whether he wanted to admit it or not, at some point in his life, going solo had not been his plan. This desire to work alone had come after the accident.

"How would I have handled this situation before?" he asked.

Her head tilted inside her helmet. A small smile flickered on her lips. "Actually, I outranked you, and I would have ordered you to wait for backup."

"Would I have followed orders?"

Nic laughed. "Not a chance. We would've

gone in together, but first…" Suddenly the map became her sole focus.

"What aren't you telling me?" Whatever it was, caused her to pull away. "What would we have done first?"

She shook her head. "It's nothing. Actually, I had forgotten all about it until now. It was just something we did. It was silly."

"Well, humor me and tell me what we did that was so silly."

She released a sigh into the cold night. "We prayed. It wasn't anything formal, or even very poignant, but we would hold hands and ask God to protect us." She shrugged and smiled slightly. "See? Silly."

Jett inhaled deeply and let it out slowly. The image she painted for him about their relationship didn't match with what he had always assumed. They were both law enforcement, and with that, he'd expected they would have been too intense and rigid to allow faith into their lives. Part of him wanted to laugh it off, but the greater part of him yearned to know more. He made the decision to let the latter thought take the lead.

He reached for the map in her hands. Holding it up, he put it down on a snowmobile.

She laughed nervously. "Don't lose that.

My recollection of the area isn't that great. I need that map."

"I won't be leaving your side, and my recollection of this area is fine." He removed his gloves and reached for her hands to do the same. Holding them in front of him, he asked, "Was it like this? Did we pray like this?"

She nodded. "Sort of."

"What am I doing wrong? How was it like?" The need to get this right burned within him.

Nic took a step closer to him. She removed his helmet and put it on the seat. Then she removed her own. "We would touch foreheads." She leaned forward and encouraged him to do the same until their heads touched. She whispered, "This feels so surreal."

"For me, too, but I'm not sure why." He swallowed hard. "Did you pray or did I?"

"You did. You always prayed," she said. "You said we would be stronger if God was our lead. That we would be unstoppable."

This side of him stunned him. No one had ever told him he had believed such things. He had so many questions, but now was not the time. They had a killer to catch, and they had danger to walk into.

"I'm not sure what to say…" he began. "I can honestly say I haven't spoken to God or prayed in any way since the accident, but I'll do my best." He closed his eyes and thought of how prayer was supposed to begin. "God? I'm told I used to pray to You, so I hope You remember me."

A deep giggle erupted from Nic. "I'm pretty sure He remembers us. He wasn't the one who stopped praying."

"Right. Okay then. We are praying for Your protection, God. Keep us safe as we head into this house to stop this man from doing any more harm. Give us the strength we need to accomplish this task. Guide us in bringing safety to our community." Jett opened his eyes and raised his head. "Was it like that?"

In the headlight of the snowmobile, he saw Nic's eyes close. "Yes. It was just like that." She stepped back and turned quickly toward the woods, putting space between them. "So, what's the plan? You know this terrain. Can we make it past the swampy area this time of year?"

Jett let her change the subject. "Something tells me we will be fine." He retrieved his gun from his holster and whistled low for Tank to jump from his box. "Stay right behind me, Nic. You ready?"

With her gun in hand, she said, "Yes, but

you can get behind me." She took the lead into the woods.

Jett gave a low whistle for Tank to stay with him. At least his dog knew how to follow orders.

The glow of the A-frame could be seen through the trees from the front. Their path stayed close to the tree line as they kept the cabin in view. The peaceful tranquility seemed wrong to Jett, knowing they were about to burst through the door. Even though he had no recollection of building the place, part of him was affronted by its current occupant's illegal activity. It felt personal, which made no sense to him.

Their boots crunched across the hard snow. They tried to keep their steps soundlessly light, but the wetland was more like ice than snow given the frozen ground beneath them. Jett hoped they weren't alerting their position. The closer they neared the A-frame, the greater their chances of being shot at.

As they came upon the backside of the cabin, the inside lights could no longer be seen as they could in the front. The blackness of the lake on the other side of the home crept up to the rear of the house.

"Stay low," he instructed Nic. "As soon as

you go in, move to the right. I'm coming in behind you, covering you."

"I've never appreciated words so much."

He could tell she was trying to make light of the situation, but she wasn't fooling him. He'd seen her trauma firsthand and knew her future was riding on this evening. Her vow to give up her gun and badge hadn't been made lightly. She would keep her word. He also knew the FBI would be losing a good agent if tonight went south for her.

"Stay in the shadows." As they stepped out of the trees, Jett suddenly felt nervous about bringing her up here. He should have had Don order her to stay back. Too much was at stake. Her job was one thing, but her being injured felt like a personal assault on him, as well. He couldn't explain the feeling. "Maybe I should go in first."

"You having doubts in my abilities, Butler?" Nic asked in a hushed whisper.

"No, I'm having doubts in my own. I don't want you to get hurt." Jett stopped Tank from going any farther with him. "Tank, stay. I can't watch you both."

I can't lose you both.

Nic halted in front of him. She turned to face him and put her hand on his wrist. "You do not have to feel responsible for me. I'm a big girl, and I am going in there on my own volition. What happens in there is my choice."

"I'm expecting an ambush."

"So am I. But we prayed, right? My mom seemed to think God would be my strength if I let Him. So let's let Him."

At his nod, she turned to continue forward.

"Do you remember the layout of the house?" he asked as they neared the door. "We're going to make a commotion when we kick it in. We have to act fast."

"This leads to the kitchen. To the right is the living room. There's a bedroom around the front and two upstairs." She glanced over her shoulder and lifted something into the air. "I have the key."

Jett smiled into the night. "I like your style. Stealth it is."

She whispered, "On three." She began to count down and on the number three, she unlocked the door and slammed it wide. Bursting inside, she moved as planned.

Jett took one step and felt pain radiate from his head. His knees buckled right before everything went black.

TWELVE

Nic went to her right just as Jett had told her to. She waited for him to follow her in, but when no sign of him emerged through the doorway, she wondered where her backup had gone. With her gun drawn, she stayed crouched beside the door, her gaze jumping left to right. Her presence was known, but for some reason she felt alone.

She dropped her head back against the wall and whispered, "Jett, where are you?"

When no response came, she turned toward the door and inched closer to it. Her breathing picked up to shallow pants, and she could feel her heart rate pulse in her head. The quick look out of the corner of her eye showed a pair of boots attached to legs sprawled on the ground. At her shock of seeing Jett unconscious, she froze.

Blasts echoed through the night, coming from outside. The doorjamb right by her head splintered, and Nic felt the wind of a bullet whizz by her face. Her ears screamed in pain, which ricocheted through her mind. The gunman was close. His shot from outside had nearly been true, missing her by mere centimeters. She had to close the door. Nothing was stopping him from coming through and taking her out at point-blank range. But to cross over to get to the door would expose her.

The screaming in her mind and the ringing in her ears had yet to subside. More than anything, she wanted to grab hold of her head to make it all stop. She had to think clearly, but the noise wouldn't let her. She wondered if she would ever hear again, but right now that was the least of her worries. She needed that door closed.

Nic glanced at the distance between her and the doorknob. She didn't think her legs would even reach to be able to hook her foot and pull it closed.

Maybe not to pull it, but to kick it.

The thought came to her mind. If she could kick the door hard enough, it might hit the wall and swing back at her. She would have mere seconds to make it work. But that's all she had anyway to live.

Nic twisted her body and pulled back her

leg. With one swift kick, she sent her leg into the door as hard as she could then shrank back into hiding. Gunshots rang out, splintering the wall across from her, but the door returned to her as planned. Once again, she kicked out to push the door closed. The last thing she saw were the soles of Jett's boots before she turned the lock in one swift movement.

Her head fell to the floor as she allowed herself a few deep breaths. The ringing in her ears seemed to have lessened, but the clamor in her mind hadn't stopped. She pressed her forehead against her arm. Then she realized the screaming wasn't coming from her head but from somewhere inside the cabin.

Nic opened her eyes and tried to look behind her. She didn't want to get up and expose herself, but someone was in this house. With her gun held at the ready, she slid across the wood floor. The doorway to the living room neared, and the source of the screaming began to also register.

It was a baby.

The high-pitched tone wasn't a sound an adult made. It mimicked a type of feline, which caused her blood to curdle. The child was in hysterics. Most likely from all the gunshots. She hoped that was what it was from and not from anything criminal. Questions of why a baby would be in Jett's cabin with Saul Hansen would have to be answered later. Right now, her only concern was to make sure the child was safe.

Nic, keeping her 9mm out in front of her, used her legs to shove herself forward into the room. The only light source came from the fireplace, which cast dancing shadows along the walls. She scanned the room right to left and saw no one. With the windows from floor to ceiling, she dared not stand.

From her position on the floor, her gaze jumped from corner to corner in search of any movement. A few pieces of furniture blocked her view of the whole room. A long couch sat haphazardly by the fire. There were a couple chairs and a folding table, as well. The only other item in the room was a box. Its size looked to be about two feet by three feet.

Would she find the baby inside?

The risk to look would put her in jeopardy. To lift her head above the window line would give the shooter a target and alert him to her whereabouts inside.

Staying low, she shimmied closer to the box. Once it was within her grasp, she pushed at it to judge its weight. It moved easily. Listening to the screams also told her the baby was not in the box, but rather behind the couch. Perhaps another box? Or someone was holding the baby.

Nic's next move couldn't be rash. If there was a person holding the baby, they could have a gun at the ready. With her view shielded from the windows, she took a moment to prepare herself for exposure. She'd lost her backup with Jett and could only hope Sheriff Stewart and the rest of the team would be here soon, if not already. She contemplated waiting, staying hidden until they arrived, but the baby was beside itself and needed comfort.

Something within Nic stirred that she would not have believed possible moments before. She had a need to offer comfort to this child that went beyond her duty as an agent. With every scream, tears pricked Nic's eyes, and she wanted to call out to tell the child that all would be okay.

Gunfire blasted from somewhere outside. With her ear trained to listen, she realized backup had arrived. Nic looked at the back door. She wondered if Jett would be safe while the shooting echoed through the night air. Did she dare go back, open the door and pull him in to safety?

Hidden low in the middle of the living room, she deliberated returning to the door or going after the child. Both choices could get her killed.

With each gunshot, the baby screeched louder. Suddenly, a window imploded. Nic covered her face and bit down on her tongue to keep from screaming. Except, a scream did occur. Knowing it was not hers, Nic now knew someone else was in the cabin. It sounded like a young woman or teenager.

"I'm an FBI agent," Nic announced steadily. "Let me help the baby."

A sniff from behind the couch told Nic the girl was scared. Still, there was no response.

"Tell me your name." She hoped the friendly approach would calm the girl. "My name is Nic Harrington. I'm here to help the baby, and I can help you, too."

Another blast from outside caused the girl to cry out.

Nic took the moment to get closer. She pulled up alongside the couch and crept toward the back of it, hoping to glimpse the girl. Just as she peered around the edge, the door behind her crashed open. Now she did scream, as did both the girl and the baby.

"Nic!" Jett called out.

"Get down!"

"Oh, thank God!" He crawled around the corner. She could make out his outline in the dim firelight. As he moved closer to the hearth, she could see his face and the blood on it. "Got hit with a rock. I'm so sorry. Are you all right?"

"Yes, but we're not alone."

"I hear that. Where's the baby?"

Nic jabbed her thumb behind her to let him know, but she also held up a hand to keep him from barreling around the corner of the couch. They had no idea if the young girl had a gun. In her frightened state, she could pull the trigger accidentally.

"Are you armed?" Nic asked the girl. "We need to help the baby, but we need to know that it's safe for us to approach you."

The girl sniffed again, and the sound of trembling could be heard in her breathing. "I—I have a gun. Mr. Hansen g-gave it to me, but I didn't want it. Honest."

"Have you cocked the gun?" Nic asked.

"Y-yes. I don't know what to do with it now. Will it go off if I let it go?" Fear came through in her voice, and even if the girl didn't mean to shoot them, accidents did kill people.

Jett pulled up close to Nic and jutted his chin to let her know he would go around the other side of the couch. Once she gave him time to get there, Nic prepared to move around the backside of the couch.

"I'm going to come to help you put the gun away safely. Can you please aim it up toward the ceiling?"

"H-how do I know you aren't going to sh-shoot me?"

"I promise you I will not." Nic put her gun on the floor and slid it to be seen by the girl. "See? I put my gun down. You will not be shot by me. Now, point your gun at the ceiling."

No response came.

"Did you hear me?" Nic asked. "I need to know if it is safe for me to come help you and the baby. That's all I want to do."

"Saul said you wanted to hurt the baby." Hesitation could be heard in the girl's voice.

"He lied to you. I don't know what he told you, but Saul is not a good man. He's actually a dangerous man."

"That's not true! He *is* a good man. He cares so much about these babies."

These babies. So there were more?

Nic couldn't fathom what kind of crime she had happened upon or for how long it had been going on. Time would provide those answers, but for now, this girl needed to be detained. Whatever she believed, it wasn't that Saul Hansen was a killer.

"I gave up my gun. You see it. I can't shoot you. Let me comfort the child before it injures itself. That's all I want to do."

"He won't stop crying." The girl sounded like she was crying herself. "I don't know how to make him stop."

Nic didn't have a way with babies, so she wasn't sure how she would, either, but she wasn't about to admit that to the girl. "I can help." She hoped. "Just point the gun at the ceiling. That's all I'm asking you to do."

The girl's voice trembled. "Okay, I'm pointing it—ah!"

As soon Nic heard the girl shout out, she knew Jett had moved in to apprehend her.

She bolted from her spot just in time to grab the child from the girl's arms into the safety of her own, and Jett flipped the girl onto her stomach and handcuffed her. The gun, safely removed from her grip, lay off to Jett's side.

The threat had been extinguished. At least, inside the house.

As the young girl cried onto the floor, Nic looked down at the child in her arms. His face was beet red, and the screaming had caused him to go hoarse. She couldn't remember the last time she'd held a baby, but she brought him to the crook of her neck and began to sing a soft lullaby. It was a soothing tune she remembered her mother singing to her.

As the gunshots subsided outside, all that could be heard was Nic's lullaby floating into the darkness.

Jett's head ached, but there was something about the song that soothed him. Even the baby had stopped crying. Jett glanced Nic's way, but before he could ask her what song it was, Trevor rushed into the cabin with his gun drawn. The fire had burned low, so his features were shadowed. Still, his frantic state came through in his shallow breathing. Jett didn't want the deputy taking a shot at them, so he spoke up quickly from his crouched position by the couch.

"It's safe in here," he told Trevor, staying low by the cuffed young woman. "Is the shooter still present outside? Can we turn the lights on yet?"

"The guy took off on his snowmobile. Sheriff and Mac have gone after him. I have Tank. I'd say it's safe to put the lights on, but we're not out of the woods yet."

The girl laughed.

Jett glanced at her facedown position. "Something funny?"

"No, but I hope he gets away. He's saving children."

Whatever Saul was up to, he had convinced this young woman that it was valiant. Jett reached down and lifted the girl up from under her arms. Once she was standing, he led her around to the front of the couch to take a seat. He had many questions and hoped he could get her to share more details before she lawyered up. "What's your name?"

"Tabitha."

"Full name, please. And how do you know Saul Hansen?"

"Tabitha Mayor. Mr. Hansen is my professor at the college. He's hired me to do some babysitting. He's paying me real good, too."

Jett took the seat beside her. Perhaps he could make this feel like a conversation rather than an interrogation. She might willingly share more.

Nic was sitting on the floor behind the couch, humming to the baby. If they were looking at kidnapping charges, the FBI would have to be involved. Without alerting the girl to the trouble she was in, he asked, "Do you know where this baby's parents are?"

"That's the point. They don't have parents.

Saul finds parents for them. They were heading to foster care. I had horrible foster parents, so I know he's helping these babies."

Jett wondered how many children Saul had arranged families for. "How long have you been babysitting for him?"

"I just started last week."

"When he gave you a gun, didn't you think that was an odd thing? Didn't it make you wonder if things were legit?"

She shrugged a thin shoulder. "He showed me the pictures of the families and their children. He's doing a good thing. Honest. He said the gun was just in case someone came to kidnap the baby."

Jett needed the lights on. He had to know if this girl was for real or if she was pulling his leg. Could she really be this naïve? "Trevor, hit the lights. The switches are over by the stove."

Trevor turned and walked into the kitchen. On the wall beside the stove was a panel. "Which ones?"

"The first three will be fine. Thank you."

Instantly, light flooded the living area. Two lamps came to life beside the couch, recessed lighting above the fireplace clicked on as did the lights over the breakfast nook.

"Yo, Jett, how did you know?" Trevor asked, a stunned expression on his face.

"Know what?"

"Where the panel was and which lights to turn on." Trevor walked over to the couch. "It was like you remembered or something. I mean, you didn't even hesitate."

Jett shook his head. "That's crazy. I just knew…" Jett wondered how he'd known. There had to be a valid reason that he couldn't pinpoint at the moment. Plus, he needed to focus on where this baby had come from and how many more children had been kept up here in this cabin. How long had this been going on? He doubted Tabitha, who was a recent employee, would know.

"Can you tell me who else has worked for him as a babysitter?"

"Not personally. Mr. Hansen hires new girls from his class each semester to be his assistant." She smiled proudly. "I was so excited to be selected. He's a great boss and teacher."

Jett took a deep breath and did his best to hide his displeasure at her blind allegiance. He heard Nic rise from the floor behind him. Her lullaby had ended. He couldn't see her, but the baby's silence could only mean he was fast asleep.

Nic spoke in a whisper. "I'm sorry to tell you this, but Saul Hansen is a murderer, and apparently, also a kidnapper. He is not a good man, as you may think. He has lied to you and has made you an accomplice to kidnapping. You are in a lot of trouble."

Tabitha's face paled. She looked like she might get sick. "I… I don't understand. He said he was saving these children from a life in foster care and finding families for them."

Nic came around the couch and into Jett's view. She cradled the baby in her arms and, if he didn't know better, he would have thought she was the child's mother. His mouth went dry at the sight. He tried to lick his lips while attempting to take a deep breath.

He failed.

A strange feeling swelled in his chest, making it so tight, yet he welcomed it. He couldn't place it, but it felt right. It felt familiar and joyful. It made no sense, knowing they had just uncovered a heinous crime.

He needed to focus. He forced himself to look away from Nic and back at Tabitha. "I need you to tell us how many other children there have been and where he gets them."

Tabitha appeared shaken. Her lips trembled as she shook her head. "He doesn't tell me. He just tells me they have no family and he's saving them from a life in foster care. I think some have come from Mexico, but I'm not sure."

"Do you have experience with children? Is that why he hired you?" Nic asked, her voice a low whisper over the baby. Even still, the baby stirred and let out a small cry. Nic bent to place a gentle kiss on his forehead.

Jett's head practically exploded with this hot feeling bubbling inside him.

"Nikki," he said aloud as he jumped up off the couch.

Nic lifted her head from the baby, a stunned look on her face. She shook her head a bit and said, "You okay, Jett? You don't look well. You probably have a concussion. You just called me Nikki."

That had to be it. What other explanation could he have for wanting to walk over to Nic and kiss the same lips that had just kissed the baby?

No, not Nic, but Nikki. *His* Nikki.

"I think I'm going to be sick," he rasped, backing away from her. He bumped into Trevor and jumped away from him. If he didn't get out now, he knew he would embarrass himself. He needed air to clear away whatever was happening in his head, or there would be no stopping him from reaching for her instead. He ran to the back door and welcomed the freezing cold hitting his face once he escaped. Tank jumped up and followed him out.

He could hear Trevor and Nikki calling for him. Their voices held concern. But, if they knew the truth, he would have to face it, too.

Jett knelt by the frozen lake, wrapping his trembling arms around his K-9. He glanced back at the cabin that he had built.

But now, he remembered every square foot of it…just as he remembered the amazing woman inside.

His Nikki.

THIRTEEN

"You're a natural," Trevor said to Nic as she placed the baby into the cardboard box Saul had brought up to the cabin. The child had stayed fast asleep while in her arms, and she hoped he would remain that way until they could get him down the mountain and into protective custody.

"I'm typically uncomfortable around babies. I don't have the motherly touch like my mom did." She brushed off his compliment and came to sit beside Tabitha on the couch.

Trevor laughed. "If you say so, but I would have to think Jett would disagree, too."

Nic looked to the back door and wondered where he had gone off to. "I'm sure that my motherly instinct is the least of his concerns right now. He was hit pretty hard. He obviously has a concussion. He was acting strange. Perhaps we should check on him."

"I can stay with Tabitha," Trevor offered.

"Why don't you go find him? He might be a lot more honest with you than he would be with me. He hides a lot from the men on the force."

"What does he have to hide?" Nic stood. "His life is a blank slate. Literally."

Trevor took the seat to watch Tabitha. He looked up at Nic and said, "I think he pushes us all away and acts like he doesn't need us, but it's not true. If I go out there, I don't think he'll be honest with me about his condition. He'll be all macho and say he's fine. And tell me to mind my own business."

"He'll probably tell me the same thing." She headed toward the door, not expecting anything less.

She stepped out into the frigid air. The moon shone over the lake and treetops causing a beam of light across the ice. To her right were the trees they had come through earlier. She circled around, looking for Jett, but found no one.

"Jett? You out here? Tank?" She gave a whistle. Perhaps he'd gone to find the rest of the team. He knew these mountains better than anyone and would be useful. Still, she felt a little let down that she had lost her partner tonight. She wanted to thank him and make sure he wasn't too hurt. It was just as well. Her life in the Bureau did not allow for Jett to be her partner. Technically, she was supposed to be on medical leave, not be involved in any type of takedown or investigation anyway. She could lose her badge completely if Lewis found out.

Nic walked closer to the lake. She hadn't been up here in ten years, but it was just as she remembered it. So peaceful. What Saul Hansen had done here made her sick. How dare he take what was supposed to be a loving home and turn it into a place for heinous crimes.

Child smuggling.

Black-market adoptions.

A willingness to commit murder to keep it covered up.

And paying off Les Harrington to use this place.

Nic could only hope her father had no idea what was being done up here.

I've had to do things I never thought I would.

His words turned her stomach as she looked to the sky and prayed silently for God to help her understand the darkness of this world. Why were so many bad things allowed to happen? Why did people choose to hurt others? Why did everything come down to the evil roots of money?

Nic had left here ten years ago because Sheriff Stewart had told her she was made for going after real criminals. Apparently, she hadn't needed to go far. They were right on her mountain. She had known it was Don's way of making her leave the department so Jett could heal without her around. He had wanted to protect Jett and make things easier for him. Something to do with Don and Jett's dad being military buddies. In the end, though, Jett never could return to the department. After seeing him work tonight, she wondered if he would reconsider it. But that would be up to him.

She closed her eyes, knowing it was best that she had left. She'd told the sheriff she would go, but she'd also known it was the right move for her, as well. The FBI was her home now.

"Nikki?" Jett spoke up from behind her.

She turned abruptly and smiled at him and his dog. She couldn't see his face clearly, but the shadows revealed he wasn't smiling back. "You're hurt, aren't you? Be honest with me, Jett. We need to get you to a doctor."

He said nothing. His gaze stayed locked on hers and caused her concern to deepen. She noticed his fisted hands by his sides. Something was wrong.

She took the steps between them until they were about a foot apart to search his eyes for any sign of a concussion. "Turn to the light so I can check your pupils." She reached for his face and moved his long hair out of his vision. Tilting his head toward the light of the house, she leaned in close, their faces now mere inches away from each other. "It's hard to tell, but I think... I think..." She noticed he was looking at her lips. Her gaze fell to his. "I think you'll be okay."

Jett shook his head and covered her hand that held his hair back from his face. He entwined their fingers and brought them to his lips. With his gaze locked on hers, he kissed the backs of her fingers.

Her face heated in an instant. "Jett, what are you doing?" Her question came out on a breath.

"I remember, Nikki." He kissed her fingers again. "I remember everything. I remember this place. I remember building it..." His voice cracked. His eyes filled with tears and streamed down his face. "With you."

"What are you saying?" Nic tried to step away, but he tightened his grip on her hand.

"I remember building it with you. Nikki,

I… I remember you." He dropped her hand and reached for her face with both of his. Covering her cheeks, his thumbs wiped beneath her eyes.

She hadn't even realized she was crying. "Let me go."

"I can't." He shook his head. "I don't even know how I let you go ten years ago. Ten years! We've lost ten years." He looked at her mouth again. Before she could retreat, he leaned in and claimed her lips with a desperate intensity that took her breath away.

His hands moved around her head and trailed down her back as he turned her head with his mouth and deepened the kiss. He felt so familiar. She could feel herself melting back to a time when her life had revolved around this man. She opened to him and kissed him back, gripping his coat as if he might disappear again.

Instant pain of the memory from the last time he'd pushed her away surfaced and plummeted in her stomach. She groaned at the feeling that made her nauseous. Where her fingers had gripped his coat, she now put her palms there to shove him back. She turned her face away from his and broke their connection.

"It's too late for us," she said.

"No. Please don't push me away. I love you. I know I do." Pain could be heard in his voice. It was a pain she knew all too well.

She took a moment to find her words. "You may remember the love you had for me." She faced him again. "But I am not that girl any longer. That girl went away ten years ago, and no amount of your memory returning will bring her back. You may remember you loved me—" she took a step to retreat to the house "—but all I remember is you rejecting me and the pain I had to deal with alone. That is a memory I can never forget."

Mac and Trevor took off on their snowmobiles, escorting Tabitha down the mountain on the back of Mac's larger machine. Jett had pulled his and Nic's snowmobiles up to the cabin and readied Tank's carrier to hold the baby.

"Sorry, buddy, but you'll be running down the road. No ride for you," he informed his dog. Tank whined and tilted his head.

When Mac had returned from the hunt for Saul, he had brought Tank back with him. The dog had lost Hansen's scent, and the trail had gone cold. Saul Hansen remained at large, and a menace to society. He was a murderer, kidnapper, child smuggler and who knew what else he had his grimy hands into?

Jett touched the top of his head where he had taken a hit. The wound still seeped with a trickle of blood. Stitches were most likely needed, but what this wound had opened up was so much bigger than a hole in his head.

A window to his past had just been thrown wide, and in the mere hours since he'd taken the hit, the memories were flooding back one after the other. He felt like two separate people, and didn't know which was the real Jett Butler, the one before the accident or the one after. The only thing he knew for sure was that Nikki Harrington was the only woman he had ever loved. She'd been his world before the accident, but he had hurt her. He'd never known how much until this moment. If she'd felt for him only half of what he'd felt for her, his rejection must have nearly destroyed her.

She was stronger than he was, though. Somehow, she had picked herself up and pressed on to create a successful life as a federal agent. He thought of how tough she was now, compared to how he remembered her before the accident. Nikki had always been smart and brave, but she never spent her time proving herself. That's all she did now. Had he done that to her by pushing her out of his life?

He remembered the joy and humor she would exude over the simplest of things. When did that go away? His Nikki could fix any soured day for the better. The question was if the people they both had become were better off now? The pain in his chest said no. There was more to their story. There had to be.

Being together wasn't an option for Nic, though. She'd made that clear. He would honor that. It felt wrong and it hurt, but he let those feelings remind him of how he had wounded her first. Knowing now what he'd done to her made him wish this night had never happened. Staying in the dark had provided a cover of ignorance, even if there was nothing blissful about their lives.

No, that's not true.

Jett may have chosen to live a loner's life since the accident, but Nikki hadn't. She was clearly the bravest and strongest of them both, so deserving of a medal of valor for the way she had pressed on. She may not welcome him back with open arms, but Jett would make sure the sheriff knew how vital her work had been tonight. And her FBI boss, too. Jett would make sure she was honored for her assistance.

The lights in the house went out, and the door opened. The exterior lamp beside the door showed she carried the bundled baby close to her chest. Her head tilted to protect the child from the cold.

"I think I've got everything," she said. "I could only find one of his little shoes." She passed over a single white baby shoe to him, and he put it in the carrier. "Are you sure we can't wait until morning to take him down?" she asked.

"Hansen is still at large. Sheriff says Child Protective Services is already en route to the lodge to take the baby. It's the safest choice for him They can start searching for his parents."

She nodded. "You're right. That is best." She hit the light and pulled the busted door closed as best she could.

"I'll get that fixed tomorrow. I don't know what *I* was thinking when I busted it open."

Yeah, I do. And now he knew exactly why. The woman he loved had been barricaded behind it, and all he'd been able to think about was getting to her.

His whole life had changed in an instant. Or rather, it finally made sense.

She stepped up to Tank's carrier and placed the baby inside. She secured him and covered him with the blanket Jett had put in there.

"Nikki—"

"Nic," she corrected immediately then turned and climbed onto her snowmobile. "Go first, and I'll follow behind. When you get to the fallen tree, stop and I will take the baby from the other side so you can go off road to get around. Understand?"

Jett paused at her abruptness. So formal and stiff. The federal agent has spoken. "Sure, I understand. Orders received." Apparently, this was how things would go now. The partnership was over.

She pulled on her helmet and closed the visor. With her hands at the ready, she rammed the throttle to rev, his cue to move out.

The ride down went a lot slower. With the special cargo in back, Jett maintained a safe speed, but he kept his senses alert in case Hansen backtracked to ambush them. The guy had to be spitting mad at losing his most recent income. By the time they made it around the fallen tree and back in front of the lodge, Jett was angry enough to track the guy down that night. And there was only one person who could lead him to him. Nikki, or *Nic,* wouldn't like it.

Les Harrington had some explaining to do for his part in the crimes. But as far as Jett was concerned, Les could explain it all to the courts. Jett would arrest him if he had to.

Nic secured her snowmobile and climbed off. She came to retrieve the baby, holding him close to her neck to warm him. Her maternal response nearly threw him off his plan, but he straightened his resolve to do whatever it took to get Hansen. And at whatever cost.

"Under the circumstances with your father, I don't think you should be helping with this case," he said.

Nic scoffed. "You can't be serious," she said over the baby's head. "This is kidnapping, most likely smuggling. I am FBI, in case you have forgotten. I *will* take jurisdiction."

The early sunrise was beginning to cast a reddish glow over the mountain. It also brought out the gold flecks in Nic's red braids. Her pursed lips that he had been kissing only hours ago were now pressed tight in anger.

Trevor exited the lodge. "Good, you're back," he said, coming over to them. "A formal request to the FBI will be issued, but Nic, if you can contact your supervisor, that would be a lot faster." Jett expected Nic to agree, but instead she grew quiet. "I'm sure I don't have to tell you I need to speak to your father," Trevor said.

If she heard him, she didn't let on. In fact, she seemed a bit distracted. Whatever she was thinking about took precedence.

"Nic, if you have some information about this case, I really need you to share it with me."

"Information?" Her voice squeaked.

"These are serious crimes. I'll get a warrant if I have to, but it would be wonderful if we can work together on this openly. Please share with me what you know. We stand a better chance of catching Hansen and whoever he works with now before he hurts anyone else. Once the FBI is here, you're going to have to share what you've uncovered anyway."

She swallowed hard then cleared her throat, more nervous than ever. He didn't think he'd ever seen her so anxious. "If it's possible, can you leave me out of it?"

"Um… I'm not sure how I could do that. I'd have to lie about everything, including tonight. Including how you're holding that baby. You've been allowed to be here because of your position as a federal agent. Why the secrecy?"

Nic chewed on her lower lip and whispered, "There's got to be a way." Her words seemed more spoken to herself than to him. Whatever concerned her had brought on some kind of panic.

Jett gave Trevor a look to have him back off. The deputy shook his head in confusion and headed back to the lodge. "I'll be inside waiting for Les to return."

Once Trevor was gone, Jett faced Nic. "I can't help you if you don't tell me what's going on. What's got you looking like a deer in headlights?"

She shook her head. "It's nothing. I'll figure it out." She turned to leave, but he shot his hand out and caught her elbow. She paused and dropped her head. Her shoulders followed, defeated. It made no sense.

"Is this about your father?"

She shook her head again, this time at least four times. "I could be in a lot of trouble," she said nervously. "I've been on mandatory forced leave."

Jett took a few seconds to comprehend her words. "From the Bureau? You haven't been allowed to work..." Realization dawned on him. "You haven't been allowed to work because of your trauma and how you freeze up."

She didn't nod this time, but she didn't have to. He had the full picture. She hadn't been honest with him about her incapacities…or her orders.

"I don't believe this, Nic. The department let you take charge of this investigation. Sheriff Stewart bestowed an honor on you."

"He owed me," she said haphazardly. "It wasn't some kind of honor."

"Well, the team didn't see it that way."

"I'm sorry, you're right. I should've been honest."

"You could've gotten someone killed. Including yourself." Jett stepped in front of her and held out his arms. She looked at them and then looked away. "Give me the baby. Your work here is done."

Seconds passed into a minute, and she had yet to hand over the child. She bent her head to the baby's. "You don't understand how hard I have had to work to earn my place. Lewis wouldn't even allow me to return to show him I could do the job. I thought…" She swallowed hard. "I thought by helping with this investigation, I could prove to myself that I was ready. Then I could march into his office and be sure."

"That's a very big risk with a lot of lives at stake. Now hand me the baby."

Just then a car came careening around the corner and into the lot. It was Dahlia's red

Lexus SUV. She pulled up next to them and jumped out from the driver's seat. Leaving the door wide, she came around the car, tears streaming down her face. "He's gone!"

"Who is gone?" Nic asked.

"Les—your father. I've been looking for him for hours. He disappeared for a walk earlier."

Jett said, "He goes for walks all the time. Why are you so concerned?"

Dahlia looked at Nic. "After what happened earlier, I've never seen him so despondent. I'm worried everything has been too much for him to handle emotionally and financially."

"Are you saying you think my father is suicidal?"

Dahlia nodded sadly. "Since the helicopter crash, all he's talked about is how he's ruined. What else could he be so devastated about?"

Nic looked Jett's way, a knowing expression on her face. Her father would be ruined if he was truly involved in illegal adoptions.

"Whose baby is this?" Dahlia asked, confusion in her tear-filled voice.

Jett responded, "We don't know, but we're going to find out."

FOURTEEN

"What's this I hear about a mandatory forced leave from the Bureau?" Sheriff Stewart stood in front of Nic. She had the baby nestled in her arms, sleeping by the fire. Jett had been able to turn the power back on in this part of the lodge. It appeared someone had known how to turn it off. Trevor would lift any prints found on the box, if the guy had been dumb enough to touch it without gloves.

Nic kept her voice low but didn't cower. "Your men were never at risk. It's just something I've had to work through since I was shot. You'll be happy to know I didn't freeze up once at the cabin tonight."

"I would have been happy if you had been straight with me from the beginning. You used me, Harrington. I won't forget this. I gave you the benefit of the doubt and trusted you. I had thought with all your successes at the FBI, you would have brought a level of integrity to our little department."

"My past trauma has not cut down my work ethic. Can you say the same? I seem to recall your attempt to control a past traumatic event within the department. You may think you gave me the benefit of the doubt, but you allowed me to be part of this investigation because you owed me. Don't forget that little detail when you're thinking about this."

"How does the sheriff owe you?" Jett asked from the office door.

Both Nic and Sheriff Stewart stared at each other in silence. Perhaps it was time Jett knew the truth. Not that it would matter now. The decision for her to leave ten years ago would have happened eventually, even without the sheriff's involvement.

"It's no big deal," Stewart said. "It was a mutual decision between us. I only wanted what was best for you."

Jett left the doorway and approached the sofa. Tank followed him and looked up at the two men. Jett's eyes squinted with confusion as he looked between Nic and Stewart. "Explain yourself. What was best for me?"

Sheriff Stewart huffed. "Now is not the time to have this conversation. Protective Services will be here any moment to take the baby. We have a killer and kidnapper on the loose, and Les Harrington is missing. Can we just focus on the crimes in front of us before we dive into the past?"

Jett's head tilted. "You should know my memories are returning." His stare penetrated like daggers at each of them. "The two of you might want to come clean before I remember something different."

"You're overreacting. The decision that we made was in your best interest. You were distraught when you woke up. You needed a fresh start." Stewart referenced Nic with a wave of his hand. "She was too good for a small-town sheriff's office. Everybody knew it. Sending her on to the FBI would've happened eventually."

Jett's gaze jumped over to her, his eyes wide in quick understanding. "You left town because the sheriff asked you to?"

Nic averted his eyes and looked at the fire, swapping out one fiery furnace for another. "Well, he didn't have to twist my arm. You made it clear you didn't want me around, either. I did you both a favor."

"But maybe if you had stayed, I would have remembered you—remembered *us*—sooner." Jett gave a twisted laugh of frustration. "Instead, everyone left me. You, my parents, my brother and sister. All of you! Why would I want to remember anyone who leaves me alone to deal with such a devastating loss?"

Nic frowned as she fought tears. She shouldn't have empathy for him. But what kind of person would she be if she didn't? No one deserved to fight their way back alone after such a traumatic event.

And yet, she had been doing the same thing since her gunshot wound. She hadn't even notified her father when she was in the hospital.

"I'm sorry you had to face all of that alone. I didn't know about your family. I can't imagine what kind of reason they had for leaving you." Nic looked at him, imploring his understanding that she did feel deep sadness for him.

Sheriff Stewart cleared his throat as he eyed his phone. "If you'll excuse me, the case worker is here. I'll be right back."

"I didn't hear your phone buzz," Jett said. "Did you really just receive a text, or are you making that up to get out of here?"

"Now listen here, Jethro, we all were upset after the accident. Maybe we did things we shouldn't have, but that doesn't give you the right to attack us now."

"Then show me the message," Jett challenged.

After Sheriff Stewart pocketed his phone,

Jett nodded. "That's what I thought. There was no text. And you didn't ask only Nic to leave town. You asked my parents, as well, didn't you?"

"You have no idea what you're talking about. This conversation will go nowhere."

"Is that because my father will lie for you? After all, he owes you a few favors from your time in the military, as you've reminded me before. You probably told him you were returning the favor by watching over me in their absence. Am I right?"

Sheriff Stewart shook his head, but he had no words. No excuses came from his mouth because it appeared there weren't any.

"Why? Why would you separate my family from me? In fact, you encouraged me to push them all away, saying they were making things worse. You brought me home to live with you instead of my parents' house. It's almost like you didn't want me to…remember."

The sheriff sputtered. Then his phone buzzed. A quick glance when he took it out, and he pivoted to exit the room, slamming wooden doors behind him.

Nic was speechless at what she had just witnessed. "I—I don't know what to say. I feel…" She looked up at Jett's pained face as he yanked at the hair hanging in his eyes and pulled it back. "I feel used, and I don't understand why."

But if *she* felt manipulated, she couldn't imagine how he felt at this moment.

Jett came around the couch and sank onto it. He dropped his face into his hands. His elbows rested on his knees. So defeated.

Nic clenched her fist where it lay on her thigh. The urge to reach over and offer him comfort made no sense. But her cuddling this sweet baby didn't, either.

And it wasn't as if he was asking for comfort.

Nic understood his need to take a moment to shed a few tears. She had her times, like when she'd woken in the hospital to find she had been shot. She'd panicked, and a nurse had had to rush in to calm her. She remembered feeling embarrassed and weak at her response. But the had nurse said what Nic needed to hear to set her mind to mending.

Could she be like that nurse right now? Did she have it in her to comfort Jett? Yesterday, she would have said no, but this sleeping baby in the crook of her arm told her he somehow felt comforted by her. A thought came to her mind. Her mother's journal entry...

Had that been the difference between yesterday and these early morning hours?

"We prayed together," she said aloud. "I think it might have helped. I can't explain it, but all I know is we asked God to help us and protect us, and here we are, knowing what Hansen has been up to, and alive despite his attempts to take us out. I'm sitting here holding a baby, which is a feat in and of itself. Maybe it had something to do with God."

Jett lowered his hands and turned his head toward her. His expression twisted his face a bit and his eyes were red. "We were going to have children. You wanted three. You even named them."

"I did?" Nic couldn't fathom such a thing.

"Now who has memory loss? I would ask you what your excuse is, but I think I already know."

"You do?" She hoped he wouldn't tell her. This felt like that moment on the ski slopes, where a choice of direction would have to be made, and the only options were two risky double black diamond trails. There would be no middle-of-the-road path, and whichever one she set her skis upon, she would find loss. But which would have the greatest loss?

"When did you really decide you wanted to leave the department for the FBI?" he asked.

Nic scoffed so loudly, the baby stirred and let out a cranky sound. She placed her hand over his soft hair and rubbed his rounded back. He gurgled and went back to sleep.

She whispered, "You know very well when that happened. If you're remembering such small details as children's names, then start focusing on the memories where you told me we were over. You'll have your answer."

"That's my point. The FBI wasn't even an option until after the accident."

"The FBI was always an option, but I chose you over it. I chose a life as your partner, both in the field and in the home, instead. Now the FBI is my family."

"Is it?"

"Stop right there," she warned, feeling her temperature rise.

He shuffled to face her fully. "Hear me out. I'm not belittling the friendships you have made in the Bureau. I'm sure they feel like family, but you walked away from not only me but your flesh-and-blood father, your real family. All because of what?"

"All because I wanted to use my skills where it counted. I wanted to deal with real crimes."

"There's crime everywhere. You're holding proof of that." He glanced at the innocent child who had been used for another's financial gain. She couldn't negate his point.

Crime *was* everywhere. She didn't have to go to the FBI to find crime. Making that her reason was just an excuse.

Then why *did* she go? Why had it been so easy a choice to leave her father, town and the man she'd loved? Probably the same reason she couldn't watch her mother die, why she couldn't watch her father fall into a depression.

"I don't know how to comfort people. I know how to catch bad guys. I know how to hang from ledges. I know how to push my body to the limit and take daring chances. I face my own death head-on, but I can't face other's."

"So it's better to be alone rather than to lose someone you love later."

Nic shrugged. She looked him in the eyes. "Isn't it? Don't you do the same thing? You work alone with only your dog. Why?"

"Because I *was* the one that everyone left. Your decision to save yourself pain only caused someone else to have the pain in your wake."

Nic thought back to that day in the hospital. She'd been sitting alone in the waiting room. "After you told me we were over, I still went to the hospital. Just to be in the same building as you. I knew you wouldn't see me, but

I would go and sit in the waiting area. After about a week, Sheriff Stewart came in and told me it was best to move on. He said I should consider the FBI. I mentioned something about contacting New Mexico's field office, but he encouraged me to go higher. That's when I realized he was asking me to leave the state."

"Asking you? Or leading you to? There's a difference. I need you to think clearly and focus on exactly what he was saying that day."

"I don't need to. I knew exactly what he was doing. He wanted me to leave. It was more of a favor that he was asking me to do. It had nothing to do with boosting my career."

"Then whose?"

"I thought yours, but you never went back to the department. I never knew he asked your family to leave you, too. Everyone was distraught, and heartbroken, and fearful. He made it sound like it would be better if I left you and your family alone to deal with this. To give you time to heal. So I did. I figured you would all heal together, and you would return to the department stronger."

"That was not the case, and I need to know why. Sheriff Stewart took matters into his own hands for some unknown reason."

"Whatever his reason doesn't matter. He had a job to do. He had a department to run. I'm sure he did what he did for the department. There was no way we would have been able to work together after the accident. Neither of us would have been working at full potential. In a strange way, he was probably just trying to lead us in a positive direction that would allow us both to do the jobs we love."

"Maybe. But that doesn't explain my parents and siblings giving up within two years. He controlled everyone. It's almost as if he didn't want me to remember who I was. Even when I told him right now how I was remembering things, he didn't respond with excitement. Shouldn't that make him happy? Wouldn't he want me to remember and be pleased the memories were coming back?"

"I don't know why your parents thought leaving was best. That's going to be a conversation you need to have with them. I hope you figure it out." That was as much comfort as Nic could muster. "Right now, I need to locate my dad to find out why he would ever partner with Saul Hansen."

Jett rose from the couch. He pushed his hair away from his face again. Staring into the fire, he said, "If I learned anything tonight, it's that nothing is as it seems." He looked down at her. "I appreciate your words and your honesty. Thank you for bringing me some comfort tonight."

Nic smirked. "I don't know if I would call it comfort. That's not one of my strong suits."

Jett nodded to the baby. "I think he would disagree. He looks quite comfortable in your arms, and you look quite comfortable holding him."

Nic looked at the sweet child sleeping so soundly. She smiled at his ability to be at peace after such a tumultuous night. "He is so perfect." When she looked up to see Jett frowning, she said, "I'm sorry for what you had to learn tonight. And I *am* happy for you and for the memories coming back to you."

"The more memories that come back, the more I wish they wouldn't."

Nic tilted her head in question. "Like what?"

"Like seeing you here, holding this child, and remembering how much I loved you."

"Don't go there, Jett," she warned quietly. "We can't go back. We can only go forward on our own paths before us. I will be leaving again as soon as this case is closed and my father is found. Whether he is guilty or innocent won't change that fact, either. The only thing I learned tonight is that I'm healed. I'm ready to return to work."

The doors opened to the morning sunlight and cold, frosty air. Two men walked in with Sheriff Stewart. A woman in a heavy parka stepped inside with them.

"Nic?" Sheriff Stewart looked her way. "This here is Special Agent Foster and Special Agent Allard. They have a message for you from your supervisor."

"Lewis gave them a message for *me*? Why didn't he just call me?"

The man who identified himself as Special Agent Foster stepped up to her. She recognized his emotionless demeanor as part of the top edge as an agent. She'd been in his shoes for ten years and wore them well. She also knew he was not bringing her good news.

"Let's hear it," she said. Even from her sitting position, she heard the authority come into her voice. There would be no niceties spoken between them.

"I'm going to need your badge and gun. Your supervisor will be in touch with you about your demotion and possible termination."

"Termination?" Whatever he said after that couldn't be heard in the thrumming of blood rushing to her head. Was she being *fired*?

The woman stepped up beside her and took the baby from her arms. Without a goodbye, the child was gone from her life. After a few moments, she realized the room was empty except for the agent waiting for her gun and badge.

Nic grabbed for her belt and freed the badge. She reached behind her and removed the gun from its holster. Both had been a part of her for so long, she felt naked without them.

When she passed the items over, Foster also left the room. The message was clear. Her involvement in this case was over. She was no longer privy to any information and, quite possibly, could be considered a suspect because of her father. She knew the rules and the direction they would take the investigation in. She also remembered why she didn't offer comfort easily. Because every time she needed it, she faced an empty room.

"Why would you report Nic to the FBI? I told you about her leave in confidence." Jett followed Sheriff Stewart on his heels through the parking lot. They approached the cruiser, but as the sheriff opened his door, Jett slammed it shut from the top. "She defended you tonight. You know that? She gave your choices for sending her away the benefit of the doubt. She said you are in charge of the department and know what's best for the team. And this is how you repay her? By getting her *fired*?"

"Jethro, Nic Harrington is a big girl and knew what she was doing was wrong. She had strict orders to stay out of the field. Her supervisor also has a team to oversee and had his reasons for keeping her on leave. She is a danger to anyone she works with. I am just glad no one in the department and surrounding towns paid for her carelessness."

"She never put anyone else at risk. She said she would give up her badge and gun on her own before she did. Nic is an ethical agent, or *was*, thanks to you. She took a bullet while on duty. All she wanted was to heal so she could return to her work, but once again, you have controlled her and decided her future. First, you send her away from me, and now you take the only thing left that matters to her. She may have given you the benefit of the doubt, but I won't. Your choices sure look like some sort of vendetta against her. Or maybe your vendetta is against me. Maybe it always was."

"Don't be ridiculous. You're like a son to me. Your father and I toured together. Brothers for life. That carries over to his kids. I have always wanted what was best for you. Now, get out of my way. I need to find Les Harrington, unless you're protecting him, too."

Stewart's eyes pierced him with their anger. Jett dropped his hand from the car roof and took a step back. Something didn't feel right. The man who had been like a second father and mentor to him seemed crazed.

"I would never interfere with an investigation by shielding a suspect. The fact that you would think this of me only makes me question you and your own choices. Sheriff, have you ever interfered in an investigation by shielding a suspect?"

Stewart's lips twisted. "You go too far, Jethro."

Jett shook his head. "I'm just getting started. For ten years, I have been kept in the dark about who I am. Tonight, I learned that you played a part in that. I won't stop until I know why."

Stewart opened his door. "You just stick to doing your job, or you will be fired, too."

"Who were you protecting, Don?" Jett asked, unrelenting. "What didn't you want me to remember?"

The radio blared with the dispatcher's

voice. "All units report to the Mini-Mart on Main. Possible sighting of Harrington and Hansen."

Sheriff Stewart got into his cruiser, while Jett ran to the other side of the car and opened the passenger door to get in. "Don't think our conversation is over. When this is all over, I will be waiting for an answer."

FIFTEEN

The exterior doors to the lodge opened and let in a gust of cold air. The fire had died, but Nic still sat dazed on the sofa. All around her, Christmas decorations alluded to a time of peace and joy, but there was nothing festive about her life. There was nothing joyful to celebrate, only a life to mourn. Her future snuffed out like the dying embers before her.

"Has your father returned?" Dahlia stood at the doorway. Concern was evident in her expression and the fear in her eyes. Her typical perfect ponytail hung lopsided on her head. Her mascara was smudged, having dripped from frantic tears. "I've looked everywhere."

The fact that Nic's father had not returned only made her think he was guilty. "Dahlia, you're going to have to accept that my father has been doing something illegal and he may be running."

"That's not true. Don't be ridiculous." She

came over and sat on the couch with her. "Your father is a good man." She reached for Nick's hand that lay on her knee. Nic just stared at the woman's three rings of various stones. Ruby, sapphire and a diamond.

"Is that your diamond engagement ring?" Nic asked.

Dahlia removed her hand from Nic's and placed it in her own lap where she fiddled with the diamond on her ring finger. "Yes, he picked it out himself."

"Dahlia, that is at least a karat. For a man who is going under, don't you think a ring like that is extravagant? Didn't you wonder where he got the money?"

Dahlia frowned and her shoulders sagged. Her head dropped in defeat. "I did, believe me. But Les said I was worth every penny. He made me feel guilty for questioning his gift until I relented and accepted it. But if what you say is true, then this ring is tainted. It's contraband. I just wish… I wish we could find him."

"He can survive in the darkest of winter for days. We won't find him unless he lets us. I'm not privy to the investigation, so I don't know what they're doing to hunt him down."

"Hunt? Can't you use a different word than that? It sounds so sinister."

"Dahlia, we're pretty sure he's involved in smuggling kidnapped children and selling them. Few things are more sinister than that."

"I'm sorry, but I won't believe that until I talk to him. If I could just talk to him before the police do, I am sure I could get to the bottom of this."

Nic envied Dahlia. She didn't comprehend how Les kept so much about himself private, even from his loved ones and family. She hadn't known him long enough to understand his ways.

"I see that you really do care about my father," Nic said. "But I also see that you don't know him very well yet. He keeps a lot of himself locked up inside."

"Not to me. He shares everything with me. Whether you want to believe it or not, your father loves you deeply. He's hurt because you didn't trust him enough with your injury."

"I apologized. There's nothing else I can do. I came back, but only encountered his cold shoulder. You would think he would let it go the short time I'm here." Nic waved her hand dismissively. "But I guess now I don't have any place to be. I've got all the time in the world. Once the police find him, he won't."

Dahlia let out a wail. "In town, I saw the

police at the Mini-Mart. Maybe I could go down there and try to find him, if that's where they think he is."

"I don't think it's a wise choice to put yourself in the line of fire."

Dahlia swallowed hard. "Now I really need to find him. Would they really shoot him? Nic, you have to help me. Please."

Nic sighed and dropped her head back. "I've already lost my badge and gun for getting involved."

"Oh, honey, I'm so sorry. I am, but I just don't have your knowledge of how to track someone down. I wouldn't tell anyone that you helped me. I promise. Maybe we could use the dog."

Nic lifted her head. "Jett left his dog behind?" The idea seemed strange, but he had left her so quickly, along with everyone else. She hadn't even looked for his dog. "I just assumed Tank went with him. Where is he?"

"He's a good dog. He's sitting there outside all by himself. Just waiting for his master to come back."

Nic jumped to her feet and headed outside. Sure enough, Tank sat perfectly still by the doors.

"Come in here, Tank." She waved to the dog to come inside. When he didn't move, she stepped out to grab his collar. Still, he locked his legs tight, not willing to budge. "Jett will be back soon. Come."

The dog looked up at her. His gray-blue eyes showed his confusion at being left behind. He stared at the road in the direction the cruisers had gone. The dog wanted to work.

Nic glanced behind her and saw Dahlia in the doorway. "He won't come inside."

"We could take him to Jett. He obviously wants to be with his master."

Nic rolled her eyes. "And you obviously want to know what's going on in town."

Dahlia gave a sheepish grin. "Guilty as charged. I just want to see if I can find Les first. Don't you want to help your father? Even if it means convincing him to turn himself in."

Nic sighed, knowing she was about to give in. "We go into town to give Jett his dog. Do not get involved or in the way of what is going on down there. Do you understand?"

A huge smile spread across Dahlia's face as she nodded emphatically. "I'll get your coat." She disappeared inside and, within a minute, was back with Nic's pink jacket. "I'll drive. My truck is right here." She led the way to a red SUV with tinted windows.

Nic pet Tank to urge him forward to the

truck. "We're going to find Jett. Find Jett," she repeated. "Come. Go." She wasn't sure what command would work with him. He still would not budge. And she remembered the whistle Jett would use. Nic puckered her lips and did the best she could as she slapped her hand on her thigh. "Move," she said.

Suddenly, Tank stood on all fours and raced toward the SUV. Nic didn't know which command had worked, but was glad one of them had. Dahlia held the back door open, and he jumped in and settled on the seat.

Nic climbed into the passenger front seat and buckled in. Once Dahlia was behind the wheel, they headed down the mountain pass leading them to town.

This was the first time Nic had really been alone with Dahlia. Part of her had yet to embrace the idea of her father dating another woman besides her mom, never mind getting married. But avoiding things would not help either of them in the long run. There was a good chance they would need each other in the days ahead.

"Dahlia, I want to apologize if I have come across as unaccepting and rude to you. You obviously mean quite a lot to my father. Please know that it was nothing against you personally. This situation was new for me, and I was surprised when I came home to find him dating."

"I imagine I was a big surprise to you," Dahlia said. She cackled slightly. "I'll be honest, I was surprised when your dad asked me out. He seemed pretty set in his ways, and there didn't seem to be much room for another person in his life. But I'm glad he did. We've had a wonderful time together."

"I'm glad to hear that." Nic looked out the window at the vast open pastures. Horse fences dotted the hills in the distance and some snow covered the tall grasses. As they drove farther down the mountain and dropped in elevation, the snow disappeared to just a dusting. "I'm glad he has you. Do you have a date set for the wedding? I mean if all of this is taken care of and it's a big mistake and misunderstanding where my father is concerned."

"We actually planned for Christmas." Dahlia frowned.

Nic felt her eyes bulge. "*This* Christmas? As in two weeks from now?"

Dahlia waved a hand as if to say it was no big deal. "It's just the two of us. And, of course, you. We would love to have you if you would like to join us. We don't need anything fancy. Just some sweet vows by the tree. Doesn't that sound romantic?"

The romantic imagery came to Nic's mind. She had to admit a simple wedding by the Christmas tree with just a few friends did sound lovely. "Back when I was going to get married, we were going to do something similar. We thought about a wedding on the top of the mountain with just a couple people to witness it. Then we would ski down to our home." Nic felt the smile drift from her face. She cleared her throat. "But that was a long time ago."

"That does sound lovely. I'm not much of a skier. I'd much rather keep my feet on level ground. But it sounds like you had a partner who was compatible with your adventurous spirit."

Nic let the memories of those years come back to her as they drove on toward the center of town. She remembered how compatible she and Jett had been before the accident. Dahlia continued to talk about weddings in the future, but Nic had zoned out as her mind replayed scenes from her past.

From the back seat Tank whined. Nic turned her head to look at him. He had something in his mouth. Something white. He dropped it at his paws, and she realized it was a tiny shoe. In the next moment she realized it was the missing baby shoe. She had looked everywhere in the cabin for it but had come up empty-handed. There had to be a reasonable explanation for the shoe to be in Dahlia's car.

"Dahlia, do you have grandchildren?"

Dahlia smiled and shook her head. "Honestly, honey, I never had children at all. I couldn't have any. So no, and I do not have any grandchildren, either. Why do you ask?"

"Tank is chewing on a child's shoe. I was just wondering who it belonged to."

Dahlia tried to look in her rearview mirror to see the dog. "I have no idea how that got in my car. Maybe someone put it there?"

Nic had no reason to suspect Dahlia was lying, however, she wouldn't cross it off as impossible. She reached into the back seat and grabbed the shoe. Bringing it up front, she held it in the palm of her hand for Dahlia to see. She did her best to keep her handling to a minimum.

"When we pull up, I'll have the sheriff run it for prints. There was a shoe just like it found at the cabin. If we find matching fingerprints, we'll know who's actually behind the child smuggling. This could be what clears my father—or…convicts him."

Dahlia nodded, her face forward as she drove, her chattiness dissipating with each passing mile. She was hard to read now that her cheerfulness had subsided.

"Nic, seeing as no one knows about the shoe, I would like to keep it that way and have you put it back. Or throw it out the window, for all I care."

"I can't do that. That would be highly un-ethical of me, knowing the match for the shoe was in the cabin."

"Even if that means you put your father away in prison?"

"That will be a consequence to his choices. Not mine."

Dahlia slowed the SUV as they came to an intersection. A turn to the left would bring them to the Mini-Mart at the center of town. She stopped at the red light but did not put a blinker on.

"I'm going to ask you one more time to throw that shoe out the window." Dahlia turned her head. A strange feeling emitted from her expression and there was a warning to her voice that held a lethal tone.

Nic reached for her gun. It was a reflex action whenever possible danger presented itself. Judging by Dahlia's expression and de-mand, danger had just entered in.

"Your gun is gone," Dahlia said smugly. "I made sure of it."

"*You* made sure of it? You had nothing do with it." At Dahlia's smile, Nic realized the whole scene in the lodge had been a setup. "Those men weren't FBI?" Nic asked, trying to put it all together.

Dahlia sputtered a laugh. "No, but they spend their days outwitting the FBI, so they do great impersonations. They're quite pleased with themselves at taking your gun and badge so easily. Your conscience must really be weighing on you for you to forget an agent never lets go of their gun."

What Dahlia spoke was true. Everything had happened so fast. She should have demanded to see their IDs. But at the moment, all Nic could think about was the woman from Child Services who had come in with the men.

"Sheriff Stewart brought in the two men, but he also brought in a woman."

"You betcha. She also works for me."

"But she took the baby." Nic's voice cracked at the realization that the child was back in danger.

"Of course she did. Do you have any idea how much I'll get for that kid? I wasn't about to just let him go."

A figure crossed Nic's mind. The numbers she had seen in her father's ledger. "Fifty thousand," she said. Each of the entries had been a smuggled baby.

Nic covered her mouth as her stomach revolted. "What about my father? Is he involved in this? Is this the real partnership the two of you have?"

The light turned green, but Dahlia did not take the left into town. Instead, she headed straight for the small airfield.

"Things would have gone a lot smoother for your father if you had not returned. I'll be honest, you showing up here unannounced did put a crimp in my plans for the resort. I offered to buy the place before it went under, but Les wouldn't hear of it. So, instead I offered my services to help get it back on its feet."

"Did you tell him you were going to get it back on its feet by smuggling children in his helicopter and on his land?" Nic could not fathom her father going along with this.

"Your father is not as innocent as you think. He may not have flown any children in, but he did turn a blind eye. You would be surprised how much people can be bought for. For some, it's a huge amount of money. For others, it's nostalgia. It's pride. It's the inability to let something go. Anyone who comes along and offers an opportunity to save a bit of the past has found himself a buyer who will pay anything to remain in their old ways. It's in their old ways that they feel safe."

So he knew. Nic could not deny it any longer.

"What did you say to him? Did you use my mother as a way to convince him to save the resort?"

Dahlia took the next turn into the airfield parking lot. "I didn't have to. It was self-explanatory. He would get to keep the resort and his memories of her by doing business with me. A win-win for both of us."

"Why marriage then?"

Dahlia shrugged and removed a pistol from her coat pocket. "It was an insurance policy to make sure I got my half."

Nic looked past the barrel of the gun. Across the lot, there were a few helicopters. She spotted Jett's rescue chopper, and at Tank's short gruff, she realized he'd spotted it, too.

If only she could get word to Jett. "What are we doing here? Why did you bring me to the airport?"

"You're going to go for a little ride. We have a special delivery to make. It's nice that you can join in. Unfortunately, you won't make it back."

Nic looked out to see someone already sitting in the pilot seat of one of the helicopters. "Hansen? He's expecting us? I thought we were going into town to help find my father."

"Oops, I guess I lied. I had to get you out of that lodge somehow. I made the call to the police that I witnessed Les and Saul at the Mini-Mart. All the cops are now combing that area for no reason. Meanwhile, my transaction here will go through as planned. With you and your father at the controls."

Nic looked over at the helicopter. She couldn't make out the identity of the pilot with any certainty, but if what Dahlia was saying was true, then that wasn't Saul Hansen in the seat. It was her father.

"What's your plan?" Nic asked in a low tone, knowing the woman had her in a tight spot.

"I'm glad to see you understand who's in control. I wanted the dog along in case you gave me a hard time."

Nic huffed. "You thought you could use Tank to force me to comply? He's a SAR K-9. He's not vicious. He won't attack me. He won't attack anyone."

Dahlia smiled. She was so smug. Nic curled her fists to keep from wiping it off her face. "I didn't bring him to attack," Dahlia quipped, the smile still in place. "I brought him for leverage. If you fought me, I would shoot him. Then your ex would have no one, not even his dog."

The smile fell from the woman's face, replaced with a malevolence that reflected who she was. This was now the real woman behind all the cheerfulness and helpfulness. That had all been a front.

"The Christmas decorations…" Nic said.

"What about them?"

"It was all a façade. Did you drop the bulb and smash it on purpose? So I would get shot?"

The smile was back. "Every move was planned. I have positioned people all over. And now I am positioning you into the chopper. Get going. We have a delivery to make. My last pilot wanted out. You know how that ended for him."

"The baby is in there?" Nic asked, reaching for the door handle.

"Saul found him a good family. Maybe. Who knows? I don't really care. He's got some vendetta about righting some wrong done to him in his foster home. He wants to save children from it. Whatever works, I say. It keeps him loyal to me. As long as he continues bringing in the cash, I'll use him."

Nic could hear Dahlia, but all she cared about was getting to the baby. Her mind whirled with possible ways to save him, but every idea meant getting out of this SUV and getting on that helicopter.

Then again, did she really have a choice? Both her father and the child were inside that chopper, and if she refused to join them, Tank would be shot. Nic did not doubt Dahlia's ability to fire a gun. The woman was too precise about everything.

To the authorities, this crime would appear all her father's doing. His books even showed what he'd earned by doing it.

"Does my father know you set him up?"

"He figured it out last night. When he got up to lock the office, he wasn't locking you out. He was locking me out." Dahlia's lip curled. "He crossed a line and now will pay. With you right beside him."

"So he didn't go for a walk. You had him kidnapped." Nic trembled at the image of her father being manhandled and taken against his will.

"I convinced him to move out of the private quarters to a more…let's say, 'convenient' location for my people to transfer him, if the need arose. And it did."

"You are a horrible person. You manipulated him in every way possible. He loved my mother more than anything in this world, and you even took the home they shared away from him. But I have to know…where was the ledger? I looked everywhere in that office."

Dahlia shrugged. "I'll tell ya. But then you are to open that door and get in that helicopter. Time is wasting, and the cops won't stay on the other side of town for long. That lead will grow cold fast. Got it?"

"Sure." Did she really have a choice?

"Good. You'll get your delivery instructions on board." A twinkle of sick mischief entered Dahlia's eyes. "No one ever looks up." She pointed the gun to the roof of the SUV then back at Nic. "The book was behind the ceiling tile. Now go!"

As Nic pulled the handle and pushed the door wide, Dahlia added, "Oh, by the way, one little thing I forgot to mention. You have thirty minutes to make the drop. The helicopter will explode at that point." She pretended to think by tapping her chin. "Yeah, I think that is all. *Now* you may go."

Nic would love nothing better than to remove the cutesy demeanor this woman showed. How many had fallen for it as genuine? All Nic could do was curl her lip at the woman. "This isn't over," Nic warned.

"Thirty minutes, Nic. It will all be over in thirty minutes." Dahlia turned the gun on Tank, her message clear, and Nic didn't doubt the woman would pull the trigger without a second thought. "Ten seconds, Nic. I'm done waiting for you to decide."

Nic made it to the helicopter in eight. She didn't even take the time to shut the SUV's door. If she'd had any questions on how Dahlia manipulated people into working for her, she didn't now. The woman was an expert at figuring out a person's weakness. And no matter how hard Nic had worked to toughen her demeanor for her line of work, her need to care for people won out. She would do anything for the safety of another.

Even commit a felony.

SIXTEEN

Jett was glad he left Tank to guard the lodge. This call into town had been a false alarm. No one at the Mini-Mart could attest to seeing Saul Hansen or Les Harrington. From Sheriff Stewart's passenger seat, Jett radioed the dispatcher.

"Any word yet on who made that call?" Jett asked as the sheriff pulled onto the road to the resort. The dispatcher told him to hold.

Already the clouds were filling in over the mountain. Another storm was brewing, but it was nothing compared to the squall brewing within Jett. Because of the man beside him, Jett knew he'd be walking into the lodge to a devastated Nic. Her life had just been erased like his had been, only he would do whatever it took to get her her job back.

"Jethro, I don't expect you to understand my choices, but I'm in charge, and when I see a threat, I extinguish it. Don't think for a second Nic Harrington wouldn't have done the same thing. She didn't get to where she is by playing nice."

"That's fine, but I don't have to just accept it. I will vouch for her and talk to any person I need to, to make sure she keeps her job."

The sheriff pulled up to the front of the lodge and put the cruiser into Park. There didn't appear to be anyone around. Jett searched the area for Tank. His dog was also missing.

"Something's wrong." He swung the passenger door open and stepped out onto the packed snow. He found the doors to the lodge locked. Banging on them brought no one.

"She could be in the private quarters." Sheriff Stewart took out the key that Les had given them that first night so they could come and go. He unlocked the doors, and Jett raced inside to check the private quarters.

There was no sign of anyone on the property. Jett made his way back to the lobby just as the dispatcher's voice came through his portable radio.

"Sorry about the wait, Jett. I just got a call about a dog attack over at the airfield. Some husky attacked a lady and apparently she shot it. I'm sending someone out there now."

Jett stepped outside the lodge and looked

over to where he'd left Tank sitting in the snow. A sinking feeling caused him to rush to the sheriff's cruiser. "We gotta go."

Stewart, having already locked the door, pocketed his key, asking, "Where to now?"

"The airfield. There's a chance Tank's been shot."

"How do you know?"

"I left him here to guard the lodge. Somehow, someone's moved him."

"To shoot him?"

"We'll find out."

"Any word on who made that call?" Stewart asked as he climbed in and buckled up.

"Dispatch didn't say. She got pulled away to handle this dog incident. Something tells me we'll find out when we get there."

The sheriff put the cruiser in gear and headed off in the direction of the airfield. "What makes you say that?"

"Seems all too convenient to me to have all units dispatched to one side of town only to learn it was a nothing. And now my dog has been taken and Nic is gone."

"You think your dog bit Nic and she shot him?"

"Not at all. If this husky is Tank, then he had a good reason to attack." Jett's leg bounced rapidly. "Can we put the lights and sirens on?"

Sheriff Stewart reached over and flipped the switch. He picked up speed and raced through town. Just as they approached the airfield's entrance, a helicopter flew overhead at a low clearance.

Jett looked up with concern. "He's flying way too low. Something's not right."

Stewart pulled into the lot to find a few people surrounding a woman. As they drove closer, the blond hair alerted Jett to the woman's identity. "Dahlia?"

The sheriff released a sigh. "This has got bad news written all over it." He stopped the cruiser, parked it and unbuckled. They both got out and approached the small group.

Jett searched the area for Tank, but couldn't see him nearby. "Where's the husky?"

One of the airport security men pointed to the SAR helicopter. "We put him in there. We assume he's one of yours."

Jett raced to the helicopter, but when he opened the door, Tank dashed by him and ran full-on at the group of people surrounding Dahlia.

"Tank! Stop!" For the first time ever, the K-9 disobeyed him. Jett ran after him, but there was no way he would catch him before he reached his target.

Dahlia could be heard screeching as Tank leaped into the air and came down on her.

Jett had no idea why Tank would attack like that. It made no sense. He reached the group and rammed through to grab his dog by his collar.

Dahlia screamed, but it wasn't a scream of pain. Rather, anger came through in her voice. "That dog is done. He will be dead before sundown." Blood dripped from where she'd pulled her arm from the grip of his mouth. The color red blossomed on her coat sleeve, and she would surely need stitches.

"Why is he after you?" Jett demanded. "I left him to keep guard over Nic. Where is she?"

"I tried to stop her," Dahlia cried. "I had no idea Les was involved in this crime against humanity. He must've convinced his daughter to help him deliver that stolen child."

Jett attempted to comprehend what Dahlia was telling him. He had assumed Les was involved, but he'd never thought Nic was part of it. "They went in the helicopter?" Jett thought of the low-flying chopper he had just seen. Something felt off. Les knew how to fly and would also know it wasn't safe to fly that low through town. Regardless of what crime they were being accused of, they were in imminent danger right now.

"Look what your dog has done to me! I'm bleeding everywhere. I want him put down right now! He is a dangerous menace!" The viciousness coming out of Dahlia was astounding.

"Tank does not attack unless he has a valid reason. I was told you shot at him. Where's your gun?"

"I was just trying to protect myself!" she shouted. "Nic left the car door open, and the dog tried to go after her in the helicopter. Then he decided to come after me. Doesn't anyone care that I'm bleeding here?"

Sheriff Stewart said, "I have already radioed for the paramedics. Trevor's pulling in now. He can help, too."

Jett was still waiting for the answer to his question. "Where is your gun?"

"I have her gun right here," a security guard stated.

Jett took one look at the Glock and asked for her permit. As Dahlia stood, Tank growled in Jett's grip. He had to hold the K-9 back with all his strength. Something about this woman was setting the husky off.

Dahlia turned as if to head back to her car. Only she didn't take two steps before she reached out and grabbed the gun from the security officer. She brought it back around and pointed it right at Tank. The whole group screamed, tripping over one another to get away.

Jett let his dog go.

In one clear jump, Tank charged full-force at Dahlia, propelling her to the ground. She dropped the gun and shrieked once again. The K-9 had her in his jowls.

"Stewart!" Dahlia yelled. "Fix this now! Kill this dog or else!"

Jett looked to Sheriff Stewart, who seemed to hesitate in his place. "Sir, please don't be hasty. There's a reason Tank is holding her down. He wouldn't do this unless he had valid motivation."

Sheriff Stewart locked his gaze on Jett and frowned. "You know I love you like a son, don't you?"

Jett nodded vigorously. "Of course, but please don't shoot my dog. He's all I have."

"I'm sorry for everything, Jethro." Sheriff Stewart closed his eyes for a moment. When he opened them, they held an edge that clearly indicated he'd made up his mind.

He was going to shoot Tank.

"Please, don't shoot him. He's just doing his job."

But no amount of pleading stopped the sheriff from walking over to where Tank held Dahlia in check with his jaw. Stewart reached down and pulled up on Tank's collar, then dragged the husky beyond the moaning woman by a few feet and sat him down. "Sit!" he ordered.

Would he shoot Tank right there in front of everybody?

Jett thought he would be sick, but he couldn't turn away. He would be with his dog right to the end, and by his partner to his very last breath.

Dahlia rolled herself over and onto to her knees. Gripping her arm and holding it gingerly, she sent fiery daggers through her gaze at Tank. "Do it," she ordered Stewart. "Do I need to remind you who's in charge?"

Jett squinted at her word choice, considering the elected sheriff worked for the people. He didn't waste time concerning himself with Dahlia, but instead, focused on the last remaining moments of his dog's life.

Sheriff Stewart walked back the three steps toward Dahlia. He reached down to help her to her feet. "You don't need to remind me of who's in charge. And, after today, it will be neither of us."

He reached behind him and grabbed his

handcuffs. "You have the right to remain silent—even though I know you won't. I'm pretty sure you'll have a lot to say, but none of it will be about me." Sheriff Stewart cuffed the woman then passed her over to Trevor. "Take her in. Kidnapping, child smuggling, illegal adoption, just to name a few."

No one moved, a shocked hush consuming the group.

"Sheriff?" Jett spoke first. "What's this all about?"

Dahlia let out the loudest cackle. It grated like nails on a chalkboard and caused a shiver to race up Jett's spine. "Go ahead, Don. Tell him. Tell Jett what you did to him."

Stewart reached up and removed his badge from his chest pocket. Quietly, he took his gun from its holster. He passed them over to Jett. "There are no explanations that I could give that would take away your pain. Ten years ago, after just being elected, I had left the pub after drinking a little too much. It was raining. I wasn't thinking clearly. The light turned yellow, but I thought I could make it. But then, I didn't see it turn red. I don't know. It happened so fast."

Jett swallowed the bile coming up his throat. "What are you saying?"

"I'm saying it was me. I hit you that night. And I ran."

Jett shook his head. "I don't believe this."

Dahlia cackled again. "Oh, believe it. I have all the proof. Even where he dumped his truck."

The missing puzzle pieces Jett had been searching for clicked into place. The reason why Nic had been encouraged to leave town. The reason his whole family had done the same. They had all taken this man's recommendations, trusting his elected authority, when all along, he'd only been covering for himself.

Jett looked at Dahlia and sneered. "And being the opportunist you are, you used him and his guilt to sell children? If I were you, I would start telling me where Nic and Les were heading. It might help when it comes time for the judge to give you your sentence."

A small smirk flipped the corner of Dahlia's mouth up. "They're heading to the top of Wheeler Peak, where they'll make the drop. But I doubt they'll have time to make it back down."

"Why is that?" Jett asked.

Dahlia dragged her answer out with some hesitation. "A...little birdie told me they might not make it. That's all I know."

Jett thought about how low Les had been flying that helicopter. Something must have been wrong with it. He looked across at Tank and pointed to the SAR helicopter.

"Tank, move."

The K-9 took off toward the chopper and was in the seat before his partner was even halfway there.

Jett didn't know what he was flying into, but when it came to Search and Rescue, he never really did. And he didn't ask questions, either. No matter the storm, he and Tank would face it head-on.

SEVENTEEN

"Pop, stay with me," Nic urged her father to remain awake. "I need your help flying this thing."

They were in the cockpit, at the controls. Right behind them sat Saul Hansen and the baby, who was strapped into a car seat. Nic had to do whatever she could to get this helicopter to the mountaintop and back down within twenty minutes. They were supposed to meet the next pilot at the peak and hand over the baby, but Nic wondered how she might land elsewhere and leave the child in a secure location.

With Saul's gun trained on her, it didn't look like there were many options.

Her father groaned, his head dropping low. Saul had beaten him badly. It appeared his left arm was broken, possibly his right leg, and definitely his nose.

"The pain is making me sick," Les said through his headset.

"I know. I'm going to get you someplace safe."

"No, you won't," Saul said, hearing their words through his headset. "You're not getting off this thing alive."

Nic thought of the pilot who had survived the crash on the mountain... Saul had shot him dead. Would he do the same to them, or would he let the explosive take them out?

Les did his best to operate the controls, but whenever she saw him drift sideways in his seat and the chopper start to dip, Nic jumped in to assist. Ahead, the mountain range drew closer, though as clouds filled the sky, the peak wasn't easily visible. Storms were looming. Her already daunting task of landing the chopper would be so much harder.

"I'm going to be sick," Les said. "You'll have to take over."

Nic glanced back at Saul. "I can't fly this thing. Neither can he. You're going to have to help."

Saul shook his head and waved his gun.

Nic looked to the baby and then at Saul. "If you don't help, then we all go down. If you really care about giving this child a better life than you had, then switch places with my father and help me fly this thing."

After a moment, he motioned with his gun for Les to climb into the back. When Les passed him, Saul kicked at his bad leg. Les cried out and fell onto the back seat.

As Saul took the seat in the cockpit, Nic did her best to bite her tongue at his cruelness. She hoped she would have a chance to take him in. Of course, that would mean she had to have her badge to do so. She didn't think Lewis would mind.

Once in control, Saul throttled the helicopter to a higher elevation. He took it into wispy clouds, which caused a bit of turbulence.

As Nic looked out the window at the tops of the trees, she thought about the last helicopter. How the pilot had been able to use the treetops to break his fall. Nic knew if she tried to do that, Saul would shoot her. And with the baby on board, that was too great a risk. The best thing she could do would be to land on the pad and get the baby and her father out of the helicopter. Then she could take the chopper to a more remote place to let it explode. But leaving her father with Saul at the peak would keep him in danger.

A call blared on the radio, demanding a response. Saul ignored it and kept flying upward. A second call came on the radio, but this time Saul reached over and turned it off.

Just as they neared Wheeler Peak, Nic looked out her window to see another helicopter coming their way. Its blue-and-white colors told her it was a Search and Rescue chopper. That could only mean Jett was at the controls. But what could he do for them if he was in his own helicopter and they were in this one?

"Have you landed a chopper before?" she asked Saul.

"I've been in them enough times to have figured it out. I'm sure I can land it on the pad. After that, it's all you. I don't suggest you wait too long to get it back in the air before it blows. You wouldn't want to cause an avalanche."

Nic thought of all the skiers on the slopes. Her father's Wild Mountain Ski Resort may be closed, but none of the others were. There would be no controlling an avalanche and, with the amount of snow recently, it wouldn't take much to cause a shift in the layers.

Nic didn't know how Dahlia had figured out the best way to manipulate her, but it had worked. The woman had known she would put her own life in danger if it meant another was safe.

"I want my father to live," she said. A quick look to the rear and he looked nearly passed out in his seat. But her words seemed to have stirred him slightly. He lifted his head and shook it in his groggy state. "He needs to be in a hospital."

Saul laughed. "I wanted to put him out of his misery, but Dahlia said no. For some reason, giving your father death would be welcomed by him. Perhaps seeing you blown to bits will work. Then I can kill him."

There was so much to process in Saul's statement. Besides the man's sick enjoyment at taking a life, her heart ached for the fact that her father welcomed death. She knew this wasn't a recent feeling, but rather extended back twenty years to when he'd lost his wife. For so long, he'd pushed through each day doing the best he could without the woman he loved beside him.

His despondency had put a wedge between them that had only pushed father and daughter further apart with each passing year... Until Nic had put her own wedge into the mix, accelerating their estrangement to the point she'd taken him out of her file as her emergency contact.

"I'm sorry, Pop," she said, hoping he was awake enough to hear. "I may have moved for my job, but I should have worked harder to stay connected. Part of me thought you would be happier without me. I believed you didn't want me around."

Saul laughed through the headset as Les groaned through his. "Noooo," he breathed. "You were so much like…her."

Nic struggled to see how she was like her mother. "Mom was always so nurturing and gentle. I dared not have anything breakable around me."

He shook his head and grimaced. "You found your own way…to express yourself, but your hearts for people…were the same." His beathing labored, but he pushed himself to continue. "When you both cared about someone, you jumped in feet first. You wanted to care for me…but I wouldn't let you. It hurt… too much. I did this. I am the…only one… who should be sorry. Please forgive me."

"I forgive you, Pop, but don't you give up now. I'm going to get you out of this."

Saul laughed again. "He dies with you, or he dies after. Those are the only choices." He raised the gun on his far knee then put it back, and she wondered how she could confiscate it with the controls in the way.

Saul glanced to his left, drawing her attention to the blue helicopter coming up on his side. While he looked out the window, Nic inched her hand over in an attempt to swipe the weapon.

In an instant, Saul's right hand released the control and latched onto her wrist. He squeezed it so hard, she knew it was about the snap.

Nic shouted out in agony as she tried to pry his grip from her wrist. She felt the helicopter dip as she fought for release. "Okay! I won't do it again!"

Saul let her arm go to work the controls as the helicopter headed into a tailspin. But suddenly he was being pushed sideways and slammed into the side window of the cockpit. Her father, attacking from behind, had somehow rendered Saul cataleptic.

As Nic reached for the gun, she saw that Les had used his headset helmet to knock Saul out. But now, her father was also unconscious, having used up every last ounce of his energy. Given the beating he had taken from Saul earlier, there was also a good chance he was bleeding internally. She had no time to evaluate either condition. They were all about to go down.

As the helicopter tilted, the baby awoke and cried out from his safety seat. All their lives depended on her, and she had no time to think.

Feet first, her father had just said. A gentle person wouldn't be the one to call on in this case. This was a job for a bull.

But she still had to figure out how to fly.

First, Nic flipped the radio switch back on. "Mayday! Mayday!" She hoped she was giving the right call sign.

"Nic!" Jett's voice came over the airwaves. "Are you holding the controls?"

"Yes. But we're still tilting. Pop and Saul are unconscious. The baby's crying."

"You're actually doing fine, honey. I see you. You've got this." Jett's confidence didn't help much, but she appreciated his effort.

"Just tell me what to do," she cried. "And fast. There's a bomb, Jett!"

The radio went silent for a few seconds.

"Jett? Are you still there?"

"Yes, Nikki, I'm here. I won't leave you." He sounded so solemn. "All right, so keep holding the controls." He continued with step-by-step instructions to straighten the chopper out, and soon, Nic had the helicopter steady in her grip.

But now what? She still had to land and to get everyone out before the bomb exploded. She glanced down quickly to see if there was someplace to land. All she could see were the rooftops of ski lodges.

"How much time do we have?" Jett asked calmly.

Nic looked at the clock. "Fifteen minutes. I'm supposed to land on the top of Wheeler Peak. There's another helicopter waiting there to take the baby. If I leave it there, it will explode. Jett, that could cause an avalanche. I don't know where else to take it."

"I already have an idea. The remotest location I can think of is the cabin. If you can set down between the A-frame and the water, the explosion will be away from the trees and on solid ground, far from the slope. We know that no one's at the cabin."

Even though Nic realized that would be the safest place, the idea felt like the last nail in the coffin of their relationship. "I'm sorry, Jett. I know this won't be easy for you."

He was quiet for a moment before responding. "After knowing how the place has been used, I don't think I could ever go back there anyway. It would never feel right, especially without you."

Nic guided the helicopter on in silence, stabilizing the aircraft as it moved forward mile by mile.

"Nic? I want you to know that if anything

happens, I really do remember how much I loved you. How much I still love you. I'm sorry for how I treated you when all you wanted was to care for me. I shouldn't have ever pushed you away. It will be something I regret for the rest of my life."

Tears filled Nic's eyes. Those were words she'd spent ten years longing for. How many nights had she dreamed of hearing them, only to wake up and have to relive the truth again? The pain of rejection had never left her, no matter how hard she'd pushed herself in the Bureau. No promotion had ever been enough to compensate for that moment in the hospital.

She looked at the clock. Thirteen minutes left. Even if she made it to the A-frame and landed successfully, she didn't see how she would have time to get everyone off the helicopter.

"Jett?" she nearly whispered.

"I'm here." His assurance brought her peace in her final moments. Even the baby seemed to have calmed with the hum of the rotors overhead. "Follow my lead. You are going to start to climb higher in elevation. Good," he said when she followed his direction.

Nic passed over skiers oblivious to the danger above. She longed to be with them, with no cares in the world except making tracks and catching air.

"Do you remember how we would ski together?" she asked.

"'Course I do. I remember cuddling on the chairlifts to keep warm, too." She could hear his smile in his voice. "Pull back a little bit to make this crest. Just like that. Perfect."

Ten minutes.

Nic pressed her lips tight as she flew the helicopter above the dense forest. "If I get out of this, I would like to take a chairlift ride with you, if you wouldn't mind."

"It's a date," he said, but she noticed he hadn't corrected her or told her she would get out of this.

Eight minutes.

Panic began to set in. Nic's breathing shallowed and it became harder to take air into her lungs. Her last near-death experience had come from behind, but this one she would fly into head-on. Her death would be on her terms. And that gave her solace.

"I've been given an amazing opportunity to have you with me during this time, Jett," she said.

"I'm honored to help you through this. I wouldn't have it any other way."

She swallowed hard, her lips her trembling.

"Promise me that you will not be near me when this explodes."

"I told you I'm not leaving your side. I meant it."

"Jett, you have so much to do still. You have to find your family and bring them back together. They love you. You can all start again."

"I'm not leaving you. So stop asking me to."

Six minutes.

They crested the final mountaintop and the lake could be seen from her vantage point. She accelerated a bit too fast, causing the front of the chopper to tip down.

"Bring it back and level out," Jett instructed. "Slow and steady will get you there."

"I'm nearing five minutes left. If I get this helicopter down, I'm going to put the baby outside and take the helicopter back up over the water. You understand?"

"Yeah, I understand. I don't like it, but I understand. You always were the brains in this partnership."

"You always were my anchor. I love you, Jett Butler. I have always loved you. I never stopped." Her voice trembled viciously. "Would you pray with me?"

There were a few seconds of silence before

he started. "God, this is Nikki's bravest mission ever, and she needs You most to carry it out. Something I forgot about all the times we used to pray together before missions was that we would pray for Your power as our third partner. With two, we were strong. But with three, we were unstoppable. We pray for Your strength and guidance now to bring everyone to safety and out of these plans created to harm. And, God, if I could plead for a selfish request, I would like to ask for a second chance with Nikki. She is the love of my life, and we have ten years to make up for. Not to mention, I miss having her boss me around. Amen."

A laugh bubbled up in Nic's throat to mix with her tears. "Amen. Some people need more direction than others."

"Right now I'm giving the directions. You're approaching the cabin. Start to turn left to come around the front. Slow the helicopter until you're hovering, and walk it in. Good. Watch the altimeter needle for your elevation, and slowly bring it down."

Nic followed his instructions with her eyes locked on the needle until she knew the ground was right beneath her.

Two minutes.

She had two minutes to unbuckle the child,

open the door and put him outside. If she moved fast, she might be able to get her father out, too.

As soon as the runners hit the ground, she secured the helicopter and turned to the rear seat. Her plan was to put the baby outside and drag her father to lay beside him. If she had time, she would get Saul out. But out of the corner of her eye she saw Jett's SAR helicopter set down.

Nic waved frantically for him to go. He wasn't following her orders. He jumped from his helicopter and plowed through the snow toward her. No matter how much she waved him back, he headed her way.

He reached her and pointed at his helicopter. He wanted her to take the baby to his chopper. There wasn't enough time before the helicopter exploded, but she did as he'd instructed.

She looked over her shoulder to see him lift her father out of her helicopter and heft him over his shoulder. He raced up alongside her then past her, to lay her father in the back of his helo. She took the baby inside and placed him beside her father, then pointed to her chopper.

Saul was still inside.

It would be so easy to climb aboard Jett's

helicopter and take off, but neither of them could make such a decision.

Jett reached down and took her hand. At his nod, they both ran back to her helicopter. Nic opened the door and pushed back the seat so Jett could grab Saul under the arms and drag him out. She helped Jett pick his legs up, and together they crutch-carried him to the SAR chopper.

Nic jumped in as Jett settled behind the controls. She struggled to close the doors even as he lifted off the ground. He hadn't gotten ten feet when the explosion rocketed them sideways toward the water. She dropped her body over the baby's safety seat and held on to the child as they were thrown to the other side.

Smoke filled the air as Jett wrestled with the controls to stabilize the helicopter.

"Hang on!" he yelled. "It might blow again when the fire reaches the gas tank."

Nic felt the helicopter spin and did her best to stay steady inside. Both Saul and her father tumbled about unsecured. Looking out the front window made her dizzy and nauseous, so she kept her eyes averted against the door until finally Jett brought the helicopter straight and flat.

Another explosion blasted through the air,

but with this one, they were far enough up that it only caused the chopper to shake. As Jett pulled them away from the lake, she glanced out the window to see the whole cabin engulfed in flames. When she looked toward the front at Jett, she saw him also looking below at all his hard work being destroyed.

Nic got to her knees and lifted the baby's seat. She made her way to the front and sat on the floor between him and Tank. She reached for Jett's hand. He turned and looked at her, a mixed expression on his face. She understood his confliction, for she had a similar one.

He gave her hand a squeeze then let go. Reaching to the front, he grabbed a headset and gave it to her.

When she put it on, they both said in unison, "I'm sorry."

They smiled through teary eyes at the mixed blessing they had just received. Gone was the symbol of their past dreams, but somehow, the dreams on their horizon had only just begun.

EIGHTEEN

Jett took a seat in the waiting room of the hospital. There was only one other person in there, and she seemed to be dozing in her chair across the way. He withdrew his cell phone from his belt and pulled up a number that he had never removed. Everyone else's was taken out of his contacts, but for some reason he couldn't let this one go.

Truman Butler's phone number stared at him from the screen.

The idea of making this phone call to his little brother filled him with trepidation. He couldn't possibly expect a warm welcome after skipping Thanksgiving without giving a reason. He didn't even bother a quick stop-in as he had done in the past. But he had to start somewhere.

Jett looked down the long hall to the doors of the intensive care unit. Behind them, Nikki sat bedside with her father, the two of them beginning again after years of estrangement. If it was possible for them, he hoped it would be for him and his brother, as well.

But he wouldn't know until he pressed this number.

Breath held, Jett hit the Call button.

After three rings, a familiar voice answered.

"Yeah? Is something wrong?" Tru's answer to the call wasn't exactly a warm hello, but Jett wouldn't hang up just yet.

"I guess you know it's me. Jett."

"Caller ID gave it away. What do you want?"

Jett let out a deep sigh. "I don't want anything. I… I only wanted to call and say I'm sorry. There's so much to tell you, I don't even know where to begin, but none of it matters if I first don't ask for forgiveness."

No answer came his way, and Jett wasn't even sure Tru was still there. But after a few seconds, he could hear his brother breathing.

"Anyway, something happened, and I now remember everything. I remember you all so clearly." Jett tapped his jacket where he'd apparently put something a while ago. Had it been one of the maps? he wondered. "I found one of our maps. I even used it on a case." He removed the paper from his pocket, only to see it wasn't one of the maps but rather the envelope from the town clerk's office.

Jett looked down the hallway toward the ICU as he gripped the marriage license in his hand. He had forgotten he'd put it in his coat. At the time, he hadn't known why he'd done it, but right now it was something of his past to hold on to, especially when this phone call was not going well at all.

"Like, everything? And everyone? Luci? Mom and Dad?" Tru asked.

"Right down to your favorite color."

"And what is that?" There was doubt in his brother's voice.

"Green. You always loved your Ranger green. Are you still a guide at the Caverns?" Jett asked. "I remember that's all you wanted to do. Spend your days outdoors in God's creation and telling everyone who would listen all about it."

There was silence again, until Jett could make out the unmistakable sound of crying. He sat still, allowing his brother to have a moment. His own tears prickled, and he put his fingers at the corners of his eyes to hold them back. When he opened them again, the woman on the other side of the room was staring at him. He offered her a smile to let her know everything was okay.

"I don't expect you all to welcome me back into your lives, but I do hope that some healing can happen for each of us. I truly am sorry that so much pain came out of this to so many people."

"Does Nikki know?" Tru asked, sniffling loudly.

"Yes, she's actually back in town for a little while. It's because of her that I remember you all. She's an FBI agent now. But I guess we always knew she was destined for the big leagues."

"I don't understand that. She cared more about you than any job. Do you remember how much she loved you?"

"I remember how much I loved her. If it comes even close to that, then I can't imagine the pain she felt. What you all felt."

"We only wanted you to find a life that you could love, and if that meant without us, then so be it. Have you found that life, Jett?"

The question lingered between them. Jett looked down at the envelope in his hand. "No, I haven't, but I'm hoping that will change soon. Can I ask you to contact Mom and Dad, and of course, Luci? If it's possible, I would love to see you this Christmas. But only if—"

Tru cut him off. "It's possible."

"Yeah?" Jett's heart skipped in his chest. Did he dare hope they could all begin again?

"Yeah. Count on it. Man, Dad is going to flip. In a good way, of course. Tell Nic thank you." With that, the line went dead.

Jett pocketed his phone and looked across the waiting room at the woman. She wore a smile of understanding. "God bless you," she said as Jett stood to go find Nic.

"He already has," Jett replied and headed toward the doors.

He pushed through and walked past a few rooms until he came to Les's. He stepped in quietly and found Nic's head bent over in prayer. Walking up to her, he bent his knees and joined her in silent prayer for her father's health to return fully.

After a few moments, he felt her take his hand. He opened his eyes to find her searching his face with an intense gaze.

She whispered, "What happens next?"

Jett looked at Les. "The doctor said his bones will recover. I believe he'll be home before Christmas."

She shook her head. "I was talking about us. What happens next with us?"

Jett got off his knees and sat in the chair beside hers. She'd yet to let go of his hand, and he stared at it for a moment. "I know what

I want, but I have no right to ask anything of you. I want the best for you, and I would never think that would be me. Not after everything I did."

"You weren't to blame. We know that now."

"I hurt you. That is all on me. Your forgiveness is enough for me."

Nic released his hand and reached for his face. Staring into his eyes, she asked, "What if it's not enough for me?"

"Say whatever you want, I will do it. If Lewis isn't ready to take you back and put you into the field, I will speak for you. Just say the word. I'll tell him that you are healed. That you handled yourself with amazing control in that helicopter. He would be a fool to say no."

Nic looked at her father and shook her head. "I've been gone too long already."

"I won't let you lose your job. It hasn't been that long."

"I meant I've been gone too long from here. From my home. From my father." She licked her lips and pressed them tight. "I've been gone too long from you."

A rush of air escaped Jett's lungs. "So, then, what do you want?" He could barely get the words out.

"I want… I want my partner back." She

dropped her gaze to his lips. "My partner in every way. On duty and off. On the job and for life. Is it possible, Jett? Please stop me if it's not."

He sensed panic in her voice, and all he wanted to do was to assure her that it was more than possible.

"You have given me my life back. You have given me my family back. Now, you want to give me my future back. I love you, Nikki Harrington. If you would do me one more favor, I would be forever in your debt."

"It's not a favor if we both want it."

Jett smiled as his heart filled his chest to near bursting. "If this is a dream, I don't want to ever wake up."

Les cleared his throat. "I'll second that, but I'm really hoping my little girl is sitting next to me."

Nic looked her father's way with excitement on her face. "Pop, you're awake. Yes, it's me, your little girl."

"Dahlia?" Panic covered his face.

"Going away for a long time. And so are her accomplices. It's going to be all right now. The baby is with Protective Services until all efforts are made to find his parents." She glanced Jett's way.

"We will stay in contact," Jett said. "He will always have a home."

Relief washed over her. Without taking her gaze from him, she continued, "And Pop, I think I'm here to stay." Her eyebrows arched in question. "Am I?"

Jett wouldn't miss this second chance. He got down on one knee. "Nikki, would you do me the honor of becoming my forever partner, in every aspect of our lives?"

Just then, the clicking of nails along the hallway floor could be heard, and they turned to see Tank being escorted by Mac and Trevor.

"Whoa, what have we interrupted here?" Trevor asked with a twinkle in his eye. "Does this mean you're staying, Nic?"

"She hasn't said yes yet," Jett said.

Mac said, "Well maybe this will persuade her to agree to stay. We'd like her to run for sheriff. We're pretty sure she'll win. In fact, there'll be no one running against her."

Trevor's eager eyes lit up the room. "What do you say, Nic? Will you stay?"

Jett asked, "Will you marry me?"

Tank trotted over and put his paw on their hands. He barked once.

The room erupted in laughter but quickly

died down to wait for her answer. "The pressure is intense in here," she said.

Jett smiled. "You always could handle yourself best under pressure."

Nic looked down at Tank. "Will he mind sharing his partner with me?"

"Not at all. He aims to please. Especially the people he loves the most."

Nic patted Tank's head. "And I love him." She looked up at Jett. "But not nearly as much as I love you. Yes, Jett Butler, I will marry you."

"How about Christmas Eve?" he asked, reaching into his coat pocket.

"But that's only a couple of days away. Is that even possible?"

He flashed the envelope. "It is if we have a license already. It never expires."

Joy filled the room at the prospect of a wedding that should have happened ten years ago now coming to fruition. There was something triumphant about this moment. So many wrongs were being made right. Years of pain were healing. Hope was being restored.

Nic grew quiet for a moment. She looked at her dad then around the room before stopping at Jett. "I have one condition."

"Anything. Just name it."

"This would make my mom happy, but it

will also give us the strongest marriage possible. We do nothing without God at the center. We are strong together, but we are stronger with Him in charge. He has to be the one calling the shots."

"I wouldn't have it any other way. Now, may I kiss you and seal the deal?"

A smile brushed Nic's lips and brightened her eyes. "Kiss away, Jett, and seal the deal. I'm all yours, forever and ever."

* * * * *

If you enjoyed this story,
look for these other books by Katy Lee:

Amish Sanctuary
Undercover Amish

Dear Reader,

I am so pleased that you joined Nic and Jett on their journey back to each other. It was a harrowing ride, filled with ups and downs and near-death adventures. But in the mix of all that, there were heavy topics of traumatic brain injuries and broken family relationships. It is my hope that these characters' relationships with God showed how He is at the core of all relationships, and with Him at the center leading the way, fences can be mended and healing can take place.

God bless you and thank you for reading! You can connect with me at katyleebooks. com.

Katy Lee

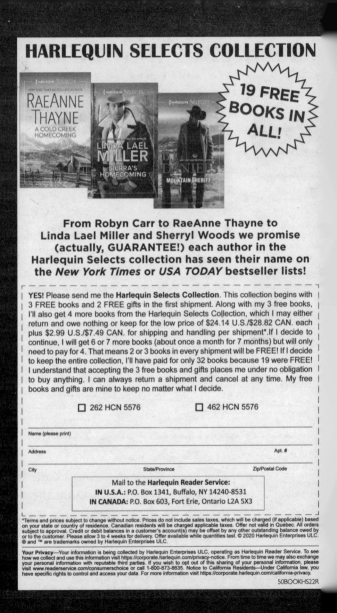

HARLEQUIN SELECTS COLLECTION

19 FREE BOOKS IN ALL!

RaeAnne THAYNE
A COLD CREEK HOMECOMING

LINDA LAEL MILLER
SIERRA'S HOMECOMING

MOUNTAIN SHERIFF

From Robyn Carr to RaeAnne Thayne to Linda Lael Miller and Sherryl Woods we promise (actually, GUARANTEE!) each author in the Harlequin Selects collection has seen their name on the *New York Times* or *USA TODAY* bestseller lists!